AMBUSHED

AMBUSHED

Bernie Ziegner

Published by **Bernie Ziegner**

ISBN: 979-8-89021-488-1 Paperback
ISBN: 979-8-89021-489-8 Hardback
ISBN: 979-8-89021-487-4 eBook

Printed in United States of America

This book is printed on acid- free paper.

Contents

Introduction

An air shipment of illicit drugs from Seattle with a street value of almost 10mil is lost in an early spring snowstorm over the Bitterroot Mountains of Idaho and Montana. The aircraft's emergency beacon was presumed to be damaged, and thus, the plane was not readily locatable. A flight plan had not been posted with the FAA, but the crew inquired about the weather en route to Missoula. Though the planned route was unknown, specific routes could be presumed when traveling from Seattle to Missoula. In the likely scenario where the maximum loaded single-engine freight hauler, Cessna 210, encountered severe wing icing, it could have been brought down rapidly in the storm. Whether the plane crashed into a peak or the pilot had chosen to fly over a lower-elevation pass is a matter of speculation.

The cargo was unknown except to a few who had every intention of mounting a recovery without public or law enforcement scrutiny. This criminal group is unable to locate the downed plane and is frantically trying every angle to get a hint as to where it might be. Two days later, news of the missing plane has gone without much notice with the residents in and around Camden. A motel manager was told of two gunshots heard by a motel guest and reported a murder to the sheriff that evening. The deceased was Samuel Henderson. The sheriff quickly discovered that this man was a DEA investigator from Salt Lake City. Also, she was told that he had spent several years for DEA in Columbia, SA. Why he was in Camden at this particular time was the question on the sheriff's mind. No one yet knew of the downed plane and that it contained illicit narcotics.

Chapter One
Missing Airplane

The eggs were sizzling in the pan. He dropped in the sausage patty. The phone rang. "Damn it, never fails."

Tom lowered the heat and reached for the wall phone without looking at the sizzling eggs.

"Hello, Tom Morrison." His grave voice gave away his irritation.

"Hi, Tom." Distracted as he was, he didn't immediately realize who was calling.

"It's Erica Stewart at the Sheriff's Office."

"Oh, good morning. I was just fixing my breakfast, I didn't look at who was calling. How's our recently elected Sheriff of Camden County?"

"Well, I do have several drunks sleeping it off here in the cages. But that's not why I called."

"What's up? We haven't talked in a couple months."

"I guess we both have been busy. The reason I called is we found a DEA agent murdered in a motel room last night. The guy's name is Henderson… Samuel Henderson."

"Henderson?"

"I was wondering if you had heard of him…in your experience with shady government agencies in Columbia or wherever."

"I do remember the name now that you mention it. But I had no direct experience with him. As I recall, he was known for recruiting spies to reveal drug organization methods regarding their shipments into the states from South America. How was he killed?"

"There were gunshots reported to the motel manager around two in the morning. After he called 911, the manager went there and used his key to gain entrance. Why in hell he didn't wait for the police is beyond me. Anyhow, inside, he found two bodies. Henderson was on his side with a bullet wound in his forehead. Next to him was a woman with a bullet wound in the back of her head. The manager said the woman was a known prostitute that hung out at the adjacent truck stop."

"Any clue as to why they were killed?"

"A couple of my deputies went there. They said the guy's personal stuff was still there, and the money was still in his wallet. It looks like an assassination."

"You think it was drug-related?"

"Don't know. I called the FBI, but I haven't heard from them. Meantime, the stiffs are at McNeil Funeral Home, and the county is getting billed."

"Strange…"

"Yeah. Meanwhile, a plane out of Seattle to Missoula has been reported missing. There was no flight plan or record of the cargo being shipped."

"Is there a search going on? Any idea where it went down?"

"Not really. The FAA said it was a Cessna 210, but they have no idea where it went down. Missoula reported they last heard from them as they started over the Bitterroot Range."

"With the stormy weather over the mountains lately, I wouldn't want to bet on them. What are you thinking?"

"I might be wrong on this, but I'm suspicious of the murder of the DEA agent at this particular time when the plane is missing. I wonder if the agent suspected it was a drug shipment. Also, was this a regular drug flight from Seattle, and they had trouble from the lousy weather up in the mountains?"

"Wow, that's a lot to ponder," said Tom. "Have you heard anything about drug deliveries coming in by plane?"

"Frankly, no. But I only have a few detectives, and they're here, not in Missoula."

"Have you heard lately from Rick?" Tom's long-time friend Rick Sherman was employed at the Bradshaw newspaper, Highland Observer. He had left town a week earlier to attend meetings in the DC area, and Tom had not heard from him.

"He hasn't called," said Erica. He should be back soon."

"I'll check with my friend Larry Johnson down in Elk Creek. He might have heard something about the plane. He…ah…hears things."

"I appreciate your doing this. Please keep me in the loop."

"Okay. Take care."

Tom hung up, not anxious to be drawn into the gossip of bygone days. He had spent over a year rebuilding the old place he had inherited from his grandparents. The previous year had been tumultuous with murder, kidnapping, drugs, violence, and, of course, there had been Lisa.

Chapter Two

Larry's Bar and Grill

Elk Creek, a small town eleven miles south of Camden, served ranch families and merchants of the area. Larry's Bar and Grill was a popular restaurant and lounge. It was just before noon when Tom parked his pickup outside Larry's and stepped into the low light of the interior. Larry, leaning his ample torso against the bar in conversation with long-time waitress Diane, turned to see Tom enter.

Larry welcomed him with a broad smile and an outstretched hand. "Hey Tom, you old dog, where have you been keeping yourself?"

They shook hands. "Staying busy working on the place. No end of things to do."

"You running any cattle out there yet?"

Tom shook his head. "Not this season. I'll buy some yearlings next spring."

"Say, you're just in time for lunch." Larry looked at Diane. "A couple cold ones and some roast beef for me and Tom."

"Sourdough?" asked Diane.

"You bet."

Diane smiled at Tom and went into the kitchen.

"Let's have a seat over by the window. Nice sun coming in."

He led Tom to the far side of the lounge, and they sat at a table. "So, Tom, what trouble have you gotten yourself into? Isn't that why you're here?"

Tom shook his head. "You know me too well. It's good to see you regardless."

"Yeah, nice to see you too. How're you and Rick doing?"

"Rick went to D.C. for something to do with the newspaper. Things have been kinda quiet lately."

"So, what's up?"

Diane brought cold draft beer and table settings. "Be a few more minutes." She smiled at Tom and went toward the kitchen.

Tom pulled his beer long and placed the wet mug on a coaster. "I received a call early this morning from the sheriff, Erica Stewart."

Larry nodded. "Nice lady."

"She told me a DEA agent had been murdered last night in a motel room along with a local gal from the truck stop. Both shot in the head."

"You got a name?"

"Samuel Henderson. Ring a bell?"

Larry ran a hand over his chin and scowled. "The name is familiar. Can't quite place him, though. What else do you have?"

"She said she called the FBI but hadn't received a call back yet."

Larry scratched his chin. "FBI and DEA…we'll see."

"Erica then told me of a small cargo plane, a Cessna 210, going in the mountains on a flight from Seattle to Missoula. It must have been the night before."

"What do we know about it?"

"There wasn't any flight plan. They were last heard from as they were about to fly over the Bitterroots."

"What about FAA? Any search set up yet?"

"They don't have a good location. Their Emergency Locator Beacon isn't working."

"Searching over that dense forest won't be easy, especially with the weather we've been getting."

"Erica and I were discussing whether it might have been a drug run from Seattle to Missoula."

Larry frowned. "Why do you say that?"

"Well, it seems rather suspicious to her. A DEA agent appears and is murdered the night after the plane disappears. We were wondering if the agent suspected it was a drug flight coming in from Seattle. They probably had trouble from the lousy weather over the mountains."

"So, this is all conjecture? No real information?"

Tom shook his head. "I decided to come see you; maybe you might have some thoughts on this."

Diane showed up with their steaming hot platters of roast beef on sourdough bread with large slices of fried potatoes.

"Thank you, Diane," Larry smiled. "Another beer when you get a minute."

Tom smiled. "Looks good. Thanks."

Diane glanced at Tom as she walked away.

"Drugs have become a real problem in these small towns," said Larry.

"We're going to lose another generation of our youth. The state can't get a handle on the distribution, and it's hard to get anyone to talk."

"What do you think about what Erica and I have discussed?"

"Ordinarily, I wouldn't put it together like that," said Larry, "but in this day and age, all the old rules don't work anymore."

"I'd like to help her out…"

Larry raised a hand and wiped his face with a napkin. "Sit tight. Finish your lunch. Diane will bring a couple more beers." He pushed his chair back and got up. "I'm going to call some folks I know on my phone in the office. Let's see what they know. I'll be back in a few minutes."

Tom watched him go toward his private office and disappear inside. Tom knew Larry kept up with his old connections in the intelligence business, and he used a particular phone for that purpose. He saw Diane approaching with two cold mugs of beer and a smile.

It was fifteen minutes later when Larry returned. He sat down, took a long pull on his beer, looked at Bob, and shook his head.

"I couldn't find much about the plane or its cargo; no one seemed to know anything. Apparently, a private crew loaded the leased plane in Seattle. The pilot and co-pilot had been hired locally but had no untoward history. The airplane had been leased to Northland Medical Group, who had been paid by bank check. I discovered no one at Northland Medical Group knew about the plane or its cargo. Furthermore, no trace of the financial transaction was recorded at Northland Medical. The whole situation with the plane seems to be some illegal transaction that might support your drug trafficking theory."

"Well, that leaves one to wonder where it is now," said Tom. "If they are carrying drugs, it's got to be a precious cargo, maybe worth more than the plane. Somebody is going to want to know where the hell it is."

"If the weather and ice brought it down over some of these high passes, it is now swallowed up by some very dense forest. I can see where this could develop into a violent confrontation between interest groups to gain access to the cargo in the plane once it's located."

"Yeah, I don't suppose anyone cares about the two pilots. The poor bastards are likely dead in the wreck," said Tom.

"You're right. No one is likely worried about the pilots except their families. Also, one could expect that the intended recipients of the cargo would pull out all the stops to find the plane."

Tom nodded. "The DEA guy must have had a tip about that plane coming into Missoula. This might not have been the first time, either. There had to have been some local guys that knew about the agent and had to get rid of him."

"Uh-huh. If your theory is correct, this could get very deadly very quickly, and I'm beginning to think it might be."

Larry got up again and went into his office. He returned with a rolled-up topographical map that he spread out on the table. He put coffee cups on the corners to hold the edges down.

"Let's suppose the pilot ran into weather and was fighting ice on the wings."

Tom nodded, "They'd be looking for a lower elevation pass to cross the Bitterroots from Idaho aiming toward Missoula."

Larry bent over the map and traced paths with his finger. "One scenario could place them south and east of your place at a lower pass where they might have tried to cross. That'd give it a straight line to Missoula."

"Erica said there's been no signal from them."

Larry sat back in his chair. "Even though other planes or satellites have not detected the emergency locator beacon, it doesn't mean it is totally non-functioning."

"What are you saying?"

"A damaged antenna in the tail section would likely make the airborne search system useless, but it might still radiate a small signal that a sensitive ground receiver could detect."

Larry got up again with a groan and went to his office. He returned with what looked to Tom as a weatherproof bag. Larry pulled out a tiny receiver and a plug-in antenna. He spent some time showing Tom how to operate the radio and how to orient the folded antenna. Tom noticed the nameplate had been removed from the drab brown radio and smiled.

"Larry, I have a horse in my barn now that could exercise. Why don't I take this and put it to use in the morning?"

Larry smiled. "That's why I showed it to you."

Tom pushed his chair back from the table.

"Hold on a minute," said Larry. "I've got something else you should take with you. I'll be right back."

Larry came back with a stiff brown envelope. "Look this over tonight and read the instructions. You'll want this to test for drugs."

"Alright, thanks. On the way home, I'll stop at the Fast Outfitter store and pick up a few things."

"How 'bout you call me when you get back?"

Tom stood up. "I will. I'll take good care of this radio."

Chapter Three

Finding the Plane Wreckage

Tom angled in to park at the front of the Fast Outfitter. This top-rated store served the ranching community with hardware, clothing, and all manner of outdoor equipment. He noticed a fancy Jeep parked nearby with every accessory likely available. Tom shook his head; more money than brains. The roof was festooned with a large light bar, and separate lights were mounted in front of the grill. Large knobby tires gave the whole vehicle a cartoonish appearance.

Curious, Tom waited. Soon, two men left the store and headed for the Jeep. He wanted a good look at them; who would own such a vehicle? He had never seen the garish vehicle before. The two men got into the Jeep. They looked white, unshaven, and in their late forties, packing fifty extra pounds. They had come out of the store wearing new field jackets and hiking boots. Tom wondered if this was one of many parties scouring the mountains for a hugely profitable drug cargo. Disgusted, he asked if anyone cared about the two pilots, whose families were likely frantic.

Inside, Tom picked up a powerful flashlight and a case of AA and DD batteries. At the register, he asked the young lady, Becky Durance, what the two men had bought. He had often favored Becky's register and admired her presence and attractive build. After hesitation and a quick glance at him, she retrieved the sales receipt and read off the items. Besides the jackets and boots, there had been a GPS compass and a box of 9mm ammunition. Their ID had shown in-state addresses in Big Fork. As he drove home, he called Erica. He told her of his conversation with Larry Johnson but omitted the particular radio part.

"Thanks for the information, but what are you going to do? I didn't mean to suggest you go chasing through the forest."

"I know. I got to thinking of the two pilots. Are they dead or alive, and does anyone give a damn?"

"Well, of course, the sheriff's department cares. I'll ask the state police to spend some time with their helicopter over the area. If they spot the wreck, I'll send a couple deputies."

"Okay. I'll ride out tomorrow morning. Let's see how far I get. I'll keep you posted on what I do."

"You have a horse now?"

"Yes. I bought a gray gelding a few months ago. I haven't exercised him much, and I'm sure he'd appreciate it."

"Horse has a name?"

"I call him Gray."

"Wow. Original."

"*I* like it."

"Okay. Take care now."

Tom was glad the conversation hadn't drifted to comments about Lisa. She was at the junior college for their two-year program, and Tom hadn't contacted her since she started there. He cared about her and thought of her often. It seemed to Tom that Erica still carried a torch for him and hadn't let go of her resentment for the young girl. Tom was glad Lisa was in junior college. However, he still thought of the beautiful forest nymph often appearing at his cabin.

By seven the following day, Tom rode Gray south through his meadow. It was a clear and cool morning, and he welcomed the chance to be in the woods. Spring flowers grew in clumps where sunlight came through the trees. He crossed the road at the end of the meadow. He went into the national forest while slipping south to approach the saddle in the eastern ridge that offered a thousand feet lower elevation than the surrounding peaks. The horse was frisky and probably glad to be away from the corral and barn. They mainly kept to well-defined elk trails, but as they neared the saddle on the ridge, they moved into dense trees, and progress became difficult. Several times, Tom had to make detours around large rock outcroppings.

Tom wore the earpiece, and the radio was clipped to his belt and set to the older emergency beacon frequency of 121.5 MHz. So far, he had only heard a soft hissing. A mile before reaching the saddle on the ridge, he listened to some undefined sounds with the ubiquitous hissing. He stopped and changed the antenna on the radio to the more directional type. As he moved the antenna, he heard what still seemed like an indefinable signal. Still, it was a little louder when he directed the antenna to the northern knob of the saddle. He changed the receiver frequency to the newer emergency beacon frequency of 406 MHz but heard a slight hiss. He switched back to 121.5 MHz. So far, he hadn't seen or heard anyone in the forest. Several crows kept announcing his arrival as he made his way toward the northern knob.

The 9mm pistol at his hip offered Tom some comfort. He grew more alert to anyone in the area as he followed the undefined signal. He knew the distress signal would have a regularity to it as it identified itself. This signal did not. But he continued to follow where the antenna pointed. He often readjusted his antenna and thus his path as he got closer to the northern knob at the pass. The signal became slightly more robust, still submerged in the noise hiss. An hour later, he reached the summit at the northern knob. The clear sky allowed a broad view over the forest, but there wasn't any trace of smoke or other clues.

As he scanned the area with the antenna, it became apparent that the signal source was not farther east but lay in his immediate vicinity. Tom scanned the forest with his powerful binoculars. Look as hard as he might; the forest didn't give up its secret. He traveled farther north on the ridgeline, and the signal seemed stronger but still embedded in the noise. He then slowly headed down the eastern slope, and when he sensed the signal to lessen, he went back up about a hundred yards. He slowly made his way south again and detected an increase in signal level. At this point, he got off his horse and proceeded on foot. He looped the reins under his belt, thus keeping the horse close to him. He couldn't sense any change in the signal as he made 90-degree treks of several hundred feet. He knew he was close, but the close spacing of the old-growth spruce and fir trees made seeing ahead nearly impossible. After almost an hour on foot, he was startled by suddenly seeing the wreck directly in front of him.

Chapter Four

Need to Protect the Wreckage

Tom stopped to look at the heading on his GPS compass. Instead of saving the data in the SAVE function of the compass, he entered the numbers into a SAVE function in his cell phone. He hoped this deception wouldn't be necessary, but one never knew; greed made people do crazy things.

He observed the plane, a Cessna 210, in an almost nose-down orientation between giant fir and spruce trees whose branches tended to smother the craft. About five feet of the tail section was torn and hung from the main body by cables and strips of torn metal. Part of the fuselage had ruptured, exposing some of the contents. When he approached closer, he saw the nose embedded in the ground. The two pilots were compressed against the instrument panel as the load behind them slammed forward at impact. They had likely died instantly. Tom recorded the tail number on his phone and the time and date. He then circled the plane, taking a photo every few feet to document the situation thoroughly.

He took photos of what he could see of the load and knelt down by some of the packaged bundles lying on the ground. He pulled one of Larry's drug test kits from his jacket pocket and reached for his penknife in his jeans. Making a small slit in the nearby suspect bundle, he slipped the knife blade into the contents and removed some of the white substance. Following the instructions that came with the test kit, he put the contents on the knife blade in the receptacle of the test kit and closed it tightly. He squeezed the test kit and shook it. The contents turned blue. Tom took pictures of the test scene and the blue indicator. There was little doubt that the white powder was cocaine. He decided not to test other different-looking bundles, fearful of what could contaminate or poison him.

He was saddened at the sight of the pilots and decided not to take photos of them in respect. Seeing that the day was moving, he climbed on his horse and headed west, down-slope, and then angled south to reach the GPS radial to his home.

Back at the corral, he rubbed down his horse, watered him, put some feed in his bucket, and went to his cabin. At the front door, he saw tracks made by knobby tires, and anger arose. He knew trouble was just starting. He walked back to the corral and locked the gate.

In the cabin, Tom locked the door and called Erica.

"Sheriff's Office, Sheriff Stewart speaking."

"Erica, this is Tom. I'm back from my survey jaunt."

"Oh, good. Did you learn anything…any luck?"

"I want to talk to you about my horseback trip."

"How about you meet me for dinner at Alfredo's? They have quiet booths. Say about six?"

"I'll see you then."

He cleaned up and activated the alarm system he had installed several years ago. A recent addition was a hi-res video recording setup activated by intruder motion. Although the violent incursions of the past were history, this new event, with the hunt for a missing plane presumed to be loaded with drugs, presented another probable crisis.

Chapter Five

Safeguarding the Cargo

During dinner, Tom told Erica of his excursion but withheld the plane's exact location.

She raised an eyebrow. "You're keeping mum on where the plane is?"

Tom sensed an edge of annoyance. "We need to secure the site from the intended cargo recipients who will certainly be looking for the plane…most frantically, I expect."

"Yes, and others would be intent on salvaging the valuable load. You did see the load?"

"Yes, I did. The fuselage had ruptured. The load looked like crates of what were probably kilos of cocaine and something else, maybe fentanyl," said Tom. "All this could present a situation of violent consequence."

Erica nodded slowly as she gazed into space. "I have to report this. Some people in the state government would want to know about this immediately…but I don't know. There's reporting protocol, but I don't want to bring political trouble to my office or me personally."

"I understand, but I'm not very sympathetic. Two bodies in that plane should be recovered as soon as possible for their families. However, I will guard the location information until a sensible plan is presented to me. Hopefully, it'll happen quickly."

"Well, what do you want me to do?"

"We must immediately establish a plan to protect the site and address the protocol reporting order."

Erica sighed and nodded. She reached for her phone. "I'll call the state attorney general, Edith Monroe. I have her unlisted emergency number."

Tom nodded. "Okay. It's a place to start."

After some discussion, Erica made plain to the AG that her source for the information would not divulge the GPS location until he was assured that the site would be protected from looters. The AG agreed that the Sheriff did not have the needed resources to protect the site. She would request from the governor an immediate state police detachment that would include Tom as part of the team and a medical examiner. The news media would be advised of the developing situation only after the state police sealed the site. The AG would also request the National Guard remove the cargo, and the fuselage using their heavy-lift helicopter and place the cargo under constant security in a National Guard building, pending the DEA's resolution of the cargo status.

After the discussion and all the phone calls, Erica and Tom relaxed to enjoy drinks and food. Tom wondered how long it would take before Erica brought up Lisa. He didn't have to wait long.

"Now, don't get antsy with me, Tom. I'm just curious: what is happening with Lisa? You and she were close a while back."

Tom took a sip of his cocktail and sighed. "She's attending Community College. She's a pretty smart girl."

"She's what, nineteen now? Do you see much of her?"

"I ran into her and her mother at the grocery store some weeks ago. She said she was doing well in her classes and hoping to get a scholarship to the University of Missoula next year."

"You help her with the tuition?"

"Her mother and I set up a trust for that."

"You're paying for it all. Aren't you?"

Tom shrugged. "They pay some of it."

She shook her head. "I've tried to understand you…"

Tom coughed and forced a smile. "They keeping you busy as the new sheriff?"

Erica sighed. "Yes, indeed. I'm not serious with anyone and can thus give fulltime to this job. The county has let me hire up to eight deputies."

"Congratulations on your well-deserved election to Sheriff. I'm sure you'll do well."

Before they departed, they promised to inform each other about events related to the downed airplane and cargo recovery.

Tom drove home and went to bed without incident. The next day, the alarm system was triggered before he finished his second coffee. He jumped out of his chair for a quick look at the window. Two Jeeps were coming to a stop in front of the cabin. One had the gaudy light strip on the roof, and when the men got out, he was sure they were the ones he had seen days before. The two men in the other Jeep remained seated in their vehicle. Tom grabbed his 9mm pistol and stuffed it under his belt before leaving the cabin.

"Howdy!" The driver tried to sound jovial.

"What are you guys doing on my property?"

"Whoa, no offense," said the driver. "We're from Stewart and Ruskin Recovery and Salvage Company and investigating sites where a plane possibly went down recently."

"Really?"

"We're interested in going through your property to access the ridge top behind you." The man gestured to the ridge west of the cabin.

"You don't say. Exploring, huh? Well, you are not welcome on my property, and besides, no plane crashed in this area."

"Sir, we've been told that the crash is likely up along that ridge somewhere. We would appreciate permission to go up there and look around."

"I don't think so. Not through my property. Find yourself differently; maybe over on the other side of the ridge."

"Is it a matter of payment? What would you charge?"

"Get the hell out of here. I'm losing my patience."

The driver suggested they would return with some legal authority as they returned to their vehicle. Tom laughed and went back into his cabin.

Chapter Six

Cargo at Risk

Late the following day, Tom e-mailed his friend Rick Sherman. He received a quick response saying he was finishing his assignment at the congressional hearing of Montana mining interests. He said he would be back in Camden in two days. Tom informed him of the plane crash and that he would talk to him about it when he returned.

Tom heard from Erica around noon.

"Hi, Erica. What's up?"

"I was just talking to the governor's office. He has yet to okay the assignment of state police to secure the downed plane site. He will demand that you relinquish the GPS data immediately to the sheriff."

"He can do that?"

"Sure, a court order."

"Without the state police securing the crash site, any leak would produce an immediate rush of criminals intent on illegally salvaging the cargo."

"I agree with you, but my hands are tied. He didn't accept the recommendations of the AG or the sheriff's office."

"This sounds a bit hokey to me," said Tom.

"Well, I hesitate to suggest the governor might have bad intentions. You should proceed cautiously."

"When it comes to money, lots of it, people look after their own interests; never mind the families of the dead pilots."

"By the way," said Erica, "I will soon be served with an order to allow an easement on your property for Stewart and Ruskin Recovery to explore the ridge line behind you. However, the order does not give them a license for any recovery."

"You've got to be kidding me. I'm sure salvage people trying to cash in on the potentially rich illicit drug cargo could well overrun my property. Hell, chief among them would be the intended recipient of the cargo, likely a deadly group of Narco criminals."

"I'm sorry, Tom. I'll give you a heads-up before something happens.

"Thanks. Let's see what tomorrow brings."

In the early evening, Tom picked up the ringing phone.

"Hello. Tom Morrison."

"Hello, Mr. Morrison. My name is Phil Sanders, and I represent the group Stewart and Ruskin Recovery."

"What can I do for you?"

"I understand a representative from our company has tried to communicate with you, and you were not inclined to hear him out. I apologize if he was rude. I am willing to pay a reasonable fee for your permission to access your property and survey the ridge line just west of your residence for evidence of a downed plane."

"Mr. Sanders, I understand what you want to do. However, I am refusing permission to you and anyone else to enter my property."

"I'm sorry, that is disappointing. I will have to pursue legal means to allow a search of the ridge behind your residence. We will be allowed access once the legal order comes through, and you will not be compensated."

Tom again refused this offer and hung up the phone. At nine o'clock, the phone rang again. Another party was seeking permission to access Tom's property in the search for a downed plane. Tom refused them as well.

Before Tom finished his breakfast the following day, Erica called and informed Tom the FAA was intent on gaining access to Tom's property, and they understood he had accurate data on the downed plane's location.

"Tell them to take a number and get in line."

"Tom, they will get their way."

"Uh-huh. Do you think the DEA should be advised of the location? It seems to me the murdered DEA agent arrived the other night with some idea as to what had been on the plane."

"I must go with what the Attorney General's office says. Ultimately, they are my boss."

"It seems to me," said Tom, "that prompt recovery of the cargo by the DEA would remove the threat of violence in the area. They're really the ones to retrieve this kind of cargo."

"It seems odd that neither the governor nor AG has said anything about the DEA being advised."

"We're talking about potentially a lot of money involved," said Tom. "Who knows what ulterior motives are at play here?"

"I don't dare contact the DEA without agreement by the AG or governor. Also, I cannot say whether *you* should or should not.»

"What about the FBI?"

"They'll be coming into town today to investigate the murder of the DEA agent. You should expect a visit from them as they are usually very thorough."

"Yeah, guess so."

"Tom, it's illegal not to tell the FBI the truth."

Tom grumbled but accepted the inevitability.

Chapter Seven
GPS Location Divulged

Tom received two more calls that morning from parties claiming to represent recovery groups interested in surveying his property for signs of the downed plane. He advised them there was no plane on his property, and they did not have permission to trespass. After noontime, the trespass alarm sounded, and an SUV boldly pulled into the yard and parked in front of his cabin.

Before Tom could grab his gun hanging on the wall, two men from the SUV entered through his unlocked door, brandishing pistols.

"What the hell…?"

"Listen, buddy, we just want to know where the plane is, and we'll be outa here."

"What the hell are you talking about? Get out of my house!"

"Hey buddy, we know you got the information. Tell us, and we're gone."

"Tell you what? I don't know about any damn plane. Now get the hell out!"

The taller of the two swung a fist at Tom's face. As he stepped back, the other man surged forward to slap Tom with the barrel of his pistol on the back of his head. The taller man pushed his gun close to Tom's face as he threatened, "Listen, bud. Stand where you are. Lou here will be looking around. Don't move."

Lou entered each room and could be heard throwing things around and cursing. He came back to stand close to his partner. "He doesn't have shit."

The taller man wiggled the gun in Tom's face. "Listen, asshole, we know you have the information we want. We'll be watching you real close." He nodded to his partner. "Let's go, Lou."

As the door closed behind the two thugs, Tom cursed himself for being careless despite the intruder alarm. In the mirror, he saw the bruises on his face and the bloody lip. He felt the knot forming on his head and cursed himself again for being careless. He thought it best to keep Erica apprised of the assault, and he called her office.

"Erica, this is Tom."

"Hello. What's up?"

"I was careless and got assaulted less than an hour ago. A couple dudes barged in here with guns."

"Christ, Tom, what did they want? Did you get hurt?"

"I got a few lumps, nothing serious. They were convinced I could tell them where the crashed plane was."

"Who were they?"

"Two white guys, middle-aged. Their SUV did not have a front tag, and I didn't see the rear plate. Oh yeah, one guy was called Lou. I don't think I heard the other guy's name."

"That's not a lot to go by. What color SUV?"

"It looked to me like a silver or gray Chevy."

"Well, I can put out an alert, but don't get your hopes up."

"I won't. I just called to let you know the bad guys are making themselves known."

"Tom, I have to apologize; although my conversation with the AG was confidential, the AG's conversation with the governor was surely not. I wouldn't be surprised if every low-life associated with the governor knows what you have discovered."

"That's just marvelous."

The following day, the FBI arrived at Tom's cabin with a DEA agent. Tom saw the government patch on their jackets as they approached the door. They were polite but forceful in their stated purpose.

"I am Special Agent Neal Anderson, and this is DEA Agent Donald Shaw." The two agents produced IDs simultaneously.

"You are Tom Morrison?"

"I am."

Agent Anderson looked carefully at Tom's face. "What happened to you? Looks like it hurts."

"A couple of guys broke in here with guns wanting the same information that you probably do. They didn't get it. I haven't told anyone about the location of any airplane wreck."

"We have to warn you, there are serious penalties for lying to the FBI," said Agent Anderson.

Tom frowned and nodded.

"We understand you know exactly where the plane is. Is this true?"

Tom showed his cell phone to the leader. "I'm recording this meeting."

Neal Anderson smiled, patted his chest, and said he was also.

"Yes, I know where it is."

"Have you been there?"

"Yes. I was there a day ago and saw it."

"What did you observe there?"

"It was a Cessna-210 nose down among tall trees. The tail section had broken off, and the fuselage had ruptured. The two pilots were smashed against the instrument panel by the load that came forward when they crashed, obviously dead."

"Did you take photos of the scene?"

"Yes. I have some on my phone." He handed Agent Anderson his phone. "You can look at them but not take my phone." The voice recorder was still turned on.

Both officers were immensely interested in the photos and viewed them several times. Agent Anderson asked Tom if he would send the images to his phone.

"I can do that. I'll send it to both of your phones."

Both agents handed Tom their phones, and in short order, both agents had copies of Tom's photos.

"Thank you for these photos. They are excellent and tell us a lot. Who else was told the exact location of this plane?"

"I told no one. I didn't want criminal looters, salvagers, or recovery people to seize the illicit drugs in the plane before DEA had a chance to remove the cargo."

DEA Agent Shaw frowned. "How do you know the cargo consists of drugs? Did you touch anything in the plane?"

"I didn't touch anything, but I'm familiar with the method of packaging drugs." Tom grinned. "I watch a lot of TV. Besides, I did a field test with a sample from one of the bundles. It's cocaine. There is a photo that shows it."

Agent Shaw nodded. "Thank you. This information is beneficial."

"How would you describe the condition of the two pilots?" asked Agent Anderson.

Tom pointed to the photos. "The cargo broke loose when they crashed and smashed them against the instrument panel. They were dead."

"Do you have the exact location of the plane?"

Tom nodded. "I do. Copied it to my phone."

"We would like to have it."

"Before I give you that, I need assurance that the site will be sealed off until the cargo and bodies are removed."

Agent Anderson nodded. "I have a team waiting in Missoula for instructions."

DEA Agent Shaw looked at Tom. "We can perform helicopter extraction of the cargo within 24 hours using local National Guard assets once the FBI seals off the area."

"We will work with local authorities," said Agent Anderson, "to process the bodies of the pilots back to their families."

Satisfied with the agreement, they shook hands, and Tom wrote them the GPS location on paper.

Tom said, "A helicopter and cargo net seems to me to be the most efficient way to remove the cargo as well as the two bodies when freed from the wreckage. There is not even an old logging road in that area. There's only dense forest."

They briefly discussed the area and terrain. Then Tom asked, "Who murdered DEA Agent Samuel Henderson?"

Both officers looked startled, apparently wondering how Tom knew the name of the dead agent. Agent Shaw shook his head. "Agent Henderson was in the area to investigate the rumor of illicit drugs coming in by plane. I didn't know him personally."

Chapter Eight

Missing Cargo

Tom called Erica and advised her of his conversation with the FBI and DEA agents. But by the afternoon of the following day, Erica still had not heard from her AG or the FBI. In her conversation with Tom that evening, they both worried about any delay allowing the criminal element to snatch the drug cargo from the plane, especially now that both the FBI and DEA had the exact location.

Tom's frustration was evident. "For crisakes, it's been almost 24 hours since I gave the location to the FBI and DEA. What about the two dead pilots? Does anyone care about them?"

"Their folks are probably ringing the alarm at the FAA and state cops," said Erica. "Won't be long before we get an army of treasure hunters looking for the damn plane if they find out there are drugs on board."

"It's maddening."

"No doubt, more bureaucratic indecision at the FBI."

"What the hell is there to argue about?" said Tom. "I gave them the location."

Erica grimaced. "Remember, the FBI, DEA, and the local National Guard are involved. You talk about indecision…"

"But it's been nearly 24 hours!"

"The National Guard unit has to agree to access the area with a large helicopter and cargo netting. And then there's the issue of cost sharing and other bureaucratic bullshit."

"Yeah. A trek through the forest by well-equipped FBI and DEA agents would take a few days. The area is heavily wooded," said Tom.

"Let's say the FBI can get themselves organized today and then another day for the National Guard and DEA to get their crap together. We'll be lucky if we hear from them by tomorrow late."

"Have you heard from the FAA?"

"No one called."

Tom was waiting to hear from the FBI or DEA the next day. However, Erica called at 4pm to relate what she had just been told by FBI Agent Howard.

"You heard from them, huh?"

"Yes, just a few minutes ago. Surprisingly, the FBI, the National Guard, and the DEA all got their stuff together, and this morning, they were at the drop site around 10am. There was plenty of sunlight by then, but it took them a while to see the downed plane."

"I told them it was nose down in the heavy timber."

"Uh-huh. They knew that. Well, they finally lowered an FBI team into a nearby clearing. Four agents made their way to the plane to discover the remains of the two pilots."

"What about the cargo?"

"As you might have guessed, except for the bodies, the fuselage was completely empty. Too much time had elapsed."

"Damn it. I told them…"

"Yeah, well, they were in a state of shock, apparently. The Special Agent in charge was lowered to assess the situation."

"Unbelievable…well, maybe not."

"The helicopter was hovering nearby all this time, using up fuel. They had to hurry."

"Did they get the pilots out of the plane?" asked Tom.

"Yes. They had brought tools with them and could pry and cut away the aluminum skin to remove them. The FBI Special Agent on site said that decomposition was evident."

"Yeah, no kidding," said Tom.

"It was evident that many shod horses had been at the site and many men trampling the ground around the plane. The pilots' bodies had not been disturbed, but every trace of cargo had been removed."

"Kiss the cargo goodbye," said Tom. "What are they going to do now?"

"The Special Agent, I forget his name, said that a well-trodden trail now existed heading east downhill from the site."

"I imagine so, what with all the horses and guys that went there while they dithered."

"Anyway, all the information was sent to the temporary FBI headquarters set up down the road from where you live on Sawmill Road. They decided to have several FBI guys track through the forest on foot on the trail left by the recovery guys and horses and find out where it ended up. Meantime, the helicopter was sent back to base with the two bodies."

"Did the FBI get to the end of the new trail?" asked Tom.

"They did. It ended up eleven miles away at the McAllister Ranch. I bet those guys were tired."

"I know the place. They rent out horses and guides during hunting season. What did the FBI say about it?"

"They found out that the recovery party had rented eight packhorses thirty hours ago and had returned five hours ago. They had loaded the cargo from the horses into a 2-ton truck and drove away. When the FBI questioned the rancher, he told them he didn't know and didn't care where they had gone or what they hauled. It had been a cash deal for $3000 to include a wrangler. The FBI interviewed the wrangler but needed to learn more of additional value. The 2-ton truck had been a non-descript, older, faded white vehicle without markings and with beat-up Montana plates. It had been seen with two men, maybe Mexican."

"Well, that is sure interesting."

"What?"

"That truck sounds like the one I saw at the Fast Outfitter," said Tom.

"Does the FBI know that?"

"Don't think so."

"Didn't you say the driver charged stuff to G&E Packaging?"

"That's what Becky Durance told me," said Tom.

"What? Who's that?"

"She works at the register at Fast Outfitter."

"She told *you,* huh?»

"I was in there buying feed."

"Whatever."

"Catch up with you later. 'Bye." Tom was anxious to get off the phone.

Special Agent Howard of the FBI visited Tom at his ranch early the following day. The agent was very agitated and angry at having lost the initiative in recovering the illicit drug cargo. Tom didn't offer any sympathy, being annoyed at the bumbling bureaucracy.

Agent Howard asked Tom, "Who do you think could pull off this operation, the McAllister Ranch guys?"

"I doubt if they had any direct responsibility in planning this heist. It presented them with an opportunity to make a few quick bucks.

Agent Howard angrily asked, "I should just ignore them?"

"They're an old outfit, and leasing horses and mules with wranglers is their business, especially in hunting season. I met the McAllister family several times and thought they were good people."

"Good people? Give me a break." The FBI special agent didn't seem convinced. "Do you think whoever is involved in the recovery could have known about the GPS location and responded this fast?"

"Well, I know the AG and the governor have been talking, and security was not likely a priority."

"It must have leaked out immediately."

"Yeah, could have. Nowadays, unless every radio conversation is encrypted, there are expert criminals around who make a business of capturing conversations and data and selling them to those who have an interest. Well-funded and aggressive criminal organizations would have no problem mounting an effort of this scale."

The agent nodded and scowled.

"I'm going to keep my task force down at the end of Sawmill Road for now."

Tom shrugged. "I don't know what else to tell you."

Chapter Nine

A White Truck

Tom was in Camden at the Fast Outfitter the next day to purchase additional feed grain. He wanted to build up a stock in his barn. It was not a busy time at the store, and he talked for a few minutes with Becky Durance at the checkout register. She was an attractive woman, he thought, maybe about thirty. He had never seen rings on her hand, so he thought to get better acquainted. They made small talk until another customer arrived, and she had to shift her attention. He hadn't been keeping company with any particular woman the past year, devoting most of his time to restoring the old homestead.

Having paid for his purchase, he proceeded to load the six fifty-pound grain sacks into his pickup. As he did so, he noticed a 2-ton white truck parked near the loading dock. Old beat-up vehicles weren't usually seen at this store. Curiosity and some suspicion deviled him until he walked over to it and looked inside the cab. It was filthy and contained scattered food containers and a pair of worn leather gloves. He could not see the registration card, so Tom walked to the back and took a photo of the dented license plate. When he returned to the store for an additional grain sack, he took the opportunity to casually walk around to look for workers who had brought the truck. He wasn't sure why he was suspicious of the car, but he had a curious itch that needed scratching.

A dark-skinned man was examining the variety of large plastic containers. The man looked like he could be of Mexican heritage. Finally, the man stacked four large containers and went to the checkout counter at the back of the store. Tom saw he paid for the containers with a credit card and then pushed through the plastic curtains to the loading dock. Tom watched the man get into the truck and drive away. Then he picked up his last sack of grain and left from the loading dock. The thought about the dark-skinned man and the white truck continued to play on his ideas. At his car, Tom pulled out his cell phone and called Erica.

"Hi, Tom. What's up?"

"Not much. I'd appreciate it if you would look up a license plate for me." He read off the number.

"Hang on a minute, looking it up now."

"I'm at the Fast Outfitter picking up some feed. My horse gets hungry."

"They all do. Okay, I've got the license report. It's expired, by the way. What do you want to know?"

"What company is it registered to?"

"It is currently licensed to Danny Silva, Property Manager, G&E Packaging and Shipping."

"What do they do?"

"Says here…a company specialized in custom packaging, machinery crates, and specialty housings. Interestingly, they claim to have a Cessna 210 leased every year for time-critical shipments. They also have three two-ton trucks for deliveries in the surrounding states."

"They do, huh?"

"This business is located in what looks like an old industrial zone from this photo, and it's a half-mile from the southern edge of the Missoula airport."

"What are you reading from?"

"It's a business directory here; it's a couple years old."

"Have you heard anything about the missing plane?"

"I asked the Seattle PD what they knew of the pilots. They said they were middle-aged men employed by G&E Packaging and Shipping of Missoula. There were no complaints or disciplinary issues on record regarding the pilots. They both worked for the company over eight years."

Tom placed the grain sacks in the wooden storage bin in the barn. He raked out the horse stall and put in clean straw. Then he grabbed some tools and tightened the leaking automatic water fountain in the horse stall. As he turned to leave, he heard the crunch of tires on the gravel just outside. Becky Durance got out of an old SUV. She smiled as she walked up to him.

"Hi Becky, nice to see you. I'm surprised."

Becky smiled as she came up to him. "I only have a minute. I'm on break."

"What's up?"

"I'm not sure what I have is important, but I recall you being very curious about the guy buying the large plastic containers."

"Yes, I was actually."

"Well, the guy just returned and purchased our whole lot of thirty. That's all of them."

"Wow. Really?"

"Yeah. I thought it rather odd. Hurried over to tell you in case it was important."

"I'm glad you did. Thank you."

"Is it…important?"

"It could be. I'll have to check up on this guy."

"The name on the credit card receipt was Jose Mendoza and was billed to G&E."

"I really appreciate your coming over."

"I tried calling you, but you didn't answer."

He thanked her again and asked her to dinner on the weekend. She accepted and drove away, saying she had to return to the store. Then he realized his cell phone was still in his truck. He always liked Becky Durance, even more now.

Yes, he thought; a purchase of over thirty plastic containers, generally sold for trash removal or grain storage, purchased by G & E was probably legitimate. On the other hand, he couldn't rid himself of the nagging thought of the white truck and dark-skinned driver. He had to check further to be sure.

Chapter Ten
G&E Packaging and Shipping

Tom considered what he knew about the strange circumstances of the downed airplane and its cargo. The plane had intended to land at Missoula, according to the fueling station operator there. Apparently, they saw that plane every other week. Now, the cargo from the downed plane had been recovered by an unknown team with the help of a hunting outfit some dozen or more miles away from where Tom lived. The cargo had then been loaded into a white 2-ton truck registered to G&E and driven away by a man named Jose Mendoza, possibly to G&E in Missoula. Today in Camden, many miles north of Missoula and a few miles west of Tom's place, a white truck with Mendoza driving stopped at the Fast Outfitter. He purchased over thirty plastic trash containers that included inner plastic bag liners. Why buy this in Camden and not in Missoula? A ruse, Tom wondered? This transaction was paid for by an account at G&E in Missoula. And presumably, Mendoza drove the white truck to G&E.

Confusing, concluded Tom. Had the illicit cargo been driven to G&E, and there it was being kept, or had it been prepared for shipment elsewhere? Was the trash containers part of this ruse? Should he convince the FBI to keep an eye on G&E in Missoula and to follow their actions with the white trucks? Missoula was out of Erica's jurisdiction. He looked at his watch. Well, just after noontime, he could make it to Missoula, check on what was happening at G&E, and hurry back to take Erica to dinner. He got into his truck and headed for the road to Missoula.

It was well after 2pm when he parked his truck where he could see the loading dock behind G&E and yet not be on their property. He saw two white trucks backed against the loading dock. He repositioned his pickup to see some of the activity on the pier. Other vehicles were parked nearby, and he felt safe from being suspected as a spy. He saw blue trash containers being hauled to the trucks with a forklift. The containers were obviously full.

Tom noticed two cars leaving the loading area and watched them disappear behind a metal building. It wasn't until a car stopped a foot in front of him that he was on full alert. As a man exited the vehicle and approached his door, he realized another car had pulled close behind him. A chill went up his back. Now, there was a man on the passenger side of his truck. Knuckles were rapping on his windows. He had the doors locked.

The glum faces outside the windows showed no emotion; they kept wrapping on the glass. Tom lowered the window on his side by about an inch and inquired what the men wanted. Suddenly the man smashed the window with the butt of a pistol and the door was quickly opened. The man grabbed Tom around the neck and yanked him out of the truck and into a heap on the ground. The second man came around the front of the car, and the two men hauled Tom to his feet. So far, the men hadn't said a word.

They quickly dragged the vociferously complaining Tom to the car in front of the truck and forced him into the back seat and next to one of the attackers. The other man was the driver, and they sped away and stopped at a nearby metal building with a small door. They forced Tom into the building and then into a small meeting room. Without anything being said, the two men started beating Tom. He fought back, but the men quickly inflicted severe harm, and Tom was totally on defense, trying to minimize the damage to his face. Suddenly, the door opened, and another man stood there with a pistol. The attackers left the room and closed the door. No one had said a word.

They left him in the room with the door closed. Tom gradually regained his composure while he sat in the single chair, and the minutes ticked by. He tried the door, but it had been locked. He noticed the din of noisy machinery had diminished. He checked his watch and realized it was after five o'clock. He had the dinner date with Erica. What would she think?

Suddenly, the door opened, and the two thugs, the apparent leader with a pistol, stood there. The other man tied Tom's wrists with a plastic Zip tie, and they shoved him out of the room. He was shoved out of the building and into the back seat of the car he had been in previously. They drove for a few minutes and stopped at what looked to Tom as an auto-wrecking yard near the railroad. Tom was pulled out of the car and forced into the car wreck. He was forced to the ground and, with additional Zip ties, was fastened to the frame of a rusted old car. He overheard one henchman mention to the other in a somewhat subdued voice that they had been told to stash him until the "stuff" was moved and the place sanitized. He didn't hear anything about letting him go, and Tom's worry increased.

Chapter Eleven

Tom Accosted

Erica paced the floor and glanced at the clock every few minutes. Had she been stood up? She thought Tom was a dependable person. He couldn't have forgotten. Was he asleep? At 6:30, she picked up her phone and called him. His phone kept ringing, and finally, he went to voice mail. She called his landline at his cabin, but here again, the call went to voice mail. Her irritation now turned to worry. He had been suspicious of the white truck and the association with G&E. She had been going to call a friend at the Missoula PD but had forgotten.

She looked through the index on her cell phone until she came to the name David Pritchard. She was relieved to see his cell phone number was listed there; sure, he would be off duty by now. She had known Pritchard for a long time. He was getting close to retirement, but he still enjoyed his work as the senior detective in the Missoula Police Department.

"Detective Pritchard."

"Hello, David, this is Erica in Camden."

"Hi. Yes, the new Sheriff. How have you been?"

"Keeping busy. Say, I have a friend here; you might have heard about him, Tom Morrison."

"Sounds familiar."

"Anyway, I'm worried as he didn't come by at 6:30 as he said he would. He is very dependable, almost to a fault. I think he might have gotten into trouble down your way. He was looking into the downed plane and the missing cargo. I don't know where he's gone with that."

"This is an FBI thing, isn't it? Why is he getting mixed up in this? He's not a cop."

"Tom had heard that the cargo in the airplane, drugs, he said, had been removed before the FBI and DEA got there. Then he heard that the stolen cargo had been taken to some ranch, loaded into a white truck belonging to G&E, and driven away. He's convinced that G&E had something to do with it and that some or all of the guys working there were involved. He was determined to check on this. I fear it may not have gone well."

"He's come down here on his own? What's he hoping to accomplish?"

"I'm not sure. It's got nothing to do with the Sheriff's office here."

"Is he some kind of hot dog?" David's voice had taken a definite edge to it.

"Kind of. He got involved with finding the plane, and now he's on some cause."

"You need to put a leash on him before he gets in trouble."

"I've got to find him first."

"Well… what can I do to help?"

"Would you mind driving by the G&E place and looking for anything suspicious? Tom owns a rusty red pickup."

"That company was bought out a couple years ago and has now gained a reputation in the PD as not being above board in their dealings with suppliers. Although I have no direct proof, I feel the company is controlled by out-of-state mob people."

"David, do you suspect drug activity?"

He hesitated. "I have no direct evidence. Haven't had a real reason to inquire on that score."

"I'm worried…"

David let out a long breath. "Do you have a license number for the red pickup?"

"No."

"I'll check out the G&E area and call you back within an hour."

"Thank you, Dave."

Tom struggled with the Zip ties on his wrists. They were cutting into his flesh, and it had become excruciating. The wrecking yard was ghostly empty; he didn't even see a stray cat. The yard lights were still on, but maybe they were always on at night. He wondered if anyone would come by in the morning or if this was an abandoned yard section. The more he thought about it, the more convinced he became that G&E was central to the illicit drug movement in the area. He wondered how long it had been going on and how the wrecking yard was involved. The temperature was dropping as the hours passed. He only wore a sweatshirt and could feel the cold penetrate through it. The soreness in his face hadn't abated. His right eye and cheek were swollen. Some ribs felt like they were cracked. He was in pain and angry. How long would it be before someone came in here? He wanted to find the two bullies that had accosted him.

David Pritchard called Erica an hour later. "Although I haven't found your friend, I did locate his red truck. The ID in the truck confirmed it. Also, his cell phone lay on the floor. The scary thing was that the driver's side window had been smashed."

Erica was shocked and alarmed. "David, something terrible must have happened. Tom was telling me his suspicions that G&E might be involved in drug trafficking. He had no real proof, but he told me a convincing story. He was probably investigating his suspicions."

"I've requested a search warrant from the DA for the G&E property. In the meantime, I've ordered a patrol team to ask for an informal search there. Erica, don't panic; I've requested additional search teams to cast a wider net around the G&E property, out to a mile."

"David, I am apprehensive. I appreciate all you can do."

"If this Tom fellow was spying on activities at G&E and was caught at it during some sensitive event, it might have gone bad. Hopefully, we can find him before his captors decide on some drastic action."

"Thank you, David. I really appreciate your help."

Near four in the morning, a patrol car received permission to break the lock on the chain link fence at Missoula Salvage and Reclaim. The patrol officers drove up and down row after row of stacked automobile carcasses. It was another half hour before Tom was spotted tied to the frame of an old wreck. The EMT team was requested, and Tom was taken to St. Patrick's Hospital to be examined and cared for his wounds. Erica was advised of Tom's condition.

In the meantime, Detective Pritchard interviewed him. "So, you're saying what? You were parked behind the G&E plant? Doing what?"

"I wanted to see who came and went. I was pretty sure the drugs from the downed plane were taken to G&E. I wanted to see who came for them."

"So, Dick Tracy, what happened then?"

Tom was visibly chagrined by the detective's attitude, but he answered his questions. "A couple of goons surprised me and busted out my window. They grabbed me and put me in a car, took me to a metal shed nearby and tied me up, and started to beat the crap outa me."

"You got names?"

Tom shook his head. "A guy came in there with a gun and started to ask me questions. Like who I was, what I was doing there, who I was working for, and what my connection was with the DEA and FBI. The man didn't accept any of my answers. The two musclemen came back into the room and beat me for a couple more minutes.

The guy with the gun said he was convinced I was working with the DEA or FBI or the local cops, at least. The two goons came back and beat on me some more."

Detective Pritchard shook his head. "Then what happened?"

"They dragged me into a car and took me to the wrecking yard. They tied me up to a car frame and left me there. That's where your officers found me."

"What did they want? What did they say to you? Must have said something."

"Just what I told you. I didn't catch any names. I was hurting a lot."

"Yeah, you look like you got the worst of it. So, Dick Tracy, that's all you got for me?

"Sorry, I don't have anymore."

The detective left the room shaking his head. He then requested a new and more thorough search warrant for G&E to be executed at eight that morning. A drug-sniffing canine was employed. Every employee of record was interviewed, and his or her alibis were recorded for subsequent review. Pritchard's team didn't discover evidence of drug processing, but it appeared the shipping department had just been cleaned. Pritchard arranged for follow-on interviews to be held at the police station of individuals that he suspected had information not yet revealed.

Erica drove to Missoula that afternoon to visit Tom at the hospital. She was disturbed by his facial injuries and that he had a fractured rib. She listened with increased interest to the story Tom told. Later, she met with Pritchard and discussed the whole episode of the plane crash and cargo seizure by the yet-unidentified gang. She arranged for Tom's truck window to be repaired and the truck to be left at the police station. Pritchard promised to explore every lead he came across. On returning to her office in Camden, Erica stopped at Tom's place to ensure his horse had food and water.

Tom was released from the hospital the following afternoon. He called Becky from the lobby and explained what had happened to him. He promised to call her soon and take her to dinner. She hoped he would be alright and happy to have dinner with him when he felt better.

Before going home, he stopped to see Larry Johnson at Larry's Bar and Grill at Elk Creek. He told Larry the whole story, from the discovery of the plane to his trouble in Missoula. He was convinced that although sufficient direct evidence might not be found with the current searches being done by Pritchard, a drug operation was indeed central in Missoula.

"I have to agree with you on this," said Larry. "It was a slick operation to acquire the drugs from the plane. Someone with deep pockets and good organization ran the show."

"How do we expose this network without the DEA? They could be helpful…but if there is a leak somewhere…." Tom shook his head.

"Let's play it safe," said Larry. "We'll try to find out who the bad guys are. Then, we have to convince the cops in Missoula to organize a raid to capture them with the goods. The PD might want the DEA involved if for nothing more than protocol and, of course, backup."

"Let's keep thinking about it.

"Sure. Keep in touch."

Tom continued homeward but stopped at the Sheriff's office and spoke briefly with Erica, promising to take her to dinner when his rib pain subsided. When he reached home, his cell phone started buzzing.

Chapter Twelve

Rick Sherman Arrives

"Hey, Rick! You finally made it home?"

"Yeah. Did you miss me?"

"You bet. I needed someone to keep me out of trouble. I met up with Larry."

"Really, that serious? Or did you just go there for a good steak?"

"I don't guess the Highland Observer got on board yet on the plane crash and the vanished cargo."

"I heard about a plane going down," said Rick. "What're you saying about the cargo?"

"It's somewhat of a story. You may want to come over and have a beer or two."

"A beer? Bet your ass. I'll be right over." Rick disconnected.

Tom pulled out two cans of beer from the refrigerator and grabbed a bowl of pretzels. As he wiped down the kitchen table, he heard tires crushing on gravel. He took a quick look out the window and deactivated the alarm system. He opened the door, and Rick walked in. His infectious smile disappeared when he saw the bruises on Tom's face.

"Christ, you look bad. What happened, her father finally beat you up?" His smile came back.

"Shut up."

"What's her name still coming around?"

"Lisa? No, she's in Junior College."

"So, what the hell happened? You look like shit."

"Sit down, it's a long story."

From the beginning, Tom told Rick the whole story; it took two beers and half the pretzels.

"How about I write an article for the paper…that'd be okay?"

Tom nodded. "Sure, but run it by Erica first. She might want to leave a detail out in the interest of justice."

"Yes, sure. You think I should run it by Larry?"

"Definitely."

"Man, that face has got to hurt."

"It does."

"What do you want to do about it?" said Rick.

"It would seem the evidence has disappeared. I have questions about whether these flights are regularly scheduled and, if so, who in Missoula is organizing them. Also, to where do the drugs disappear? What's G&E got to do with all this?"

"I'll talk to Larry and get his thoughts."

"I would really appreciate your help on this. Erica could use some help with this, too."

"Erica? Why?"

"This all happened in Camden County."

Rick nodded. "I'll give her a call."

Rick went to Larry's Bar and Grill the following day, hoping to talk to Larry about the trouble Tom was getting into.

"Hey, good to see you again; it's been a while." Larry shook hands with Rick and signaled the waitress to a table by the window.

"Good to see you too. I just returned from a trip to D.C. Tom told me about his problems."

"Oh yes, he came by yesterday. I got the whole story. He convinced me that although direct evidence of drug trafficking at the plane or in Missoula may not be currently available, it probably had been for a time. According to Erica, a detective, Pritchard, is investigating the likelihood of a drug operation in Missoula."

A waitress brought two cold mugs of beer. "Thanks, Diane."

Rick took a deep drought and nodded. "It was a slick operation to acquire the drugs from the plane. Someone had deep pockets and a good organization."

"I sure agree with you on this," said Larry.

"When I mentioned the DEA, Tom got nervous. He's afraid any leak from them could result in someone being killed," said Rick. "But this isn't our play, is it? We're not cops."

"That's true. I agree we need to play it safe. We discussed figuring out who was running things before we got the Missoula police DEA or anyone else involved. We need to know for certain who the leaders are."

"Okay. I will write an article for the paper, see if I can stir up some action."

"We both have some good sources from our past. They might come in handy in getting a line on these characters. Let's have another beer before you leave; I haven't seen you yet."

Chapter Thirteen

Erica and Becky

Tom wore a sports jacket over a plaid snap-button shirt and clean jeans to take Erica to dinner. He was pleased to see her dressed very attractively in gray slacks, a white silk blouse, and a light sweater. Although Tom liked Erica, he had not pursued her romantically. He had to admit he had more than a passing crush on Lisa. The beautiful and vivacious too-young girl had captured his heart. He understood that Erica, a deputy sheriff at the time, had been attracted to him from the day they met. Still, he had done nothing consciously to promote it. Over a year ago, they had all been involved in an episode of criminal violence that had swept through their lives. Later, Erica had been elected Sheriff. Tom respected her and her position as Sheriff of Camden County.

Tom took Erica to Roberto's, a restaurant in Camden known for steak and seafood. They relaxed with a cocktail before addressing the issues of the day. Tom described the assault by who he presumed were men from G&E.

"The deputies in Missoula could not get anyone at G&E to give up anything on the hoodlums that assaulted you and left you tied to the old car," said Erica.

"What about the owner of the wrecking yard?" asked Tom. "What did he have to say?"

"Those guys claimed they knew nothing about you being tied up in their yard. They said it's not unusual for someone to drive into the yard. It's a big place, and it's common for people to drive there looking for car parts. The guy claimed when the workers went home, they locked the gate like they always do."

"The thugs at G&E and at the wrecking yard are all part of the same outfit," said Tom, "I'm sure of it."

Erica shrugged. "It could be, of course, but we and Missoula have nothing so far to tie it all together."

Tom shook his head. "I believe G&E is central to all this trouble. I believe they have drugs shipped in by plane every couple of weeks; they repackage it at their facility and dispense it to distributors right there at the G&E building."

Erica smiled. "Everything I know so far suggests what you say could be true. However, neither I nor Missoula has any real evidence allowing anyone to seek an indictment. They're still interviewing those G&E guys. Maybe we'll get a break."

"I'm not holding my breath."

"Tom, I'm very sorry about what happened to you. I feel somewhat responsible for sending you on the wild goose chase."

"Not your fault. Something is going on, and we barely scratched the surface. It may have been going on for a long time."

Erica nodded. "You're right. I need to get together with the Missoula police and work to get our arms around this. In the end, though, it is really their call."

They asked for another cocktail and ordered food. Meanwhile, their conversation addressed Rick's return and his intent to write an article to get the bad guys to react. Erica worried it might incite more violence to Tom and Rick.

As Tom expected, Erica eventually steered the conversation to her curiosity about Lisa and what Tom's continuing ties might be.

"She used to ride her horse over the ridge to visit you often, as I recall," said Erica.

Tom nodded slowly. "She did."

She looked at him. "Don't you miss that?"

Tom shrugged. "It was fun having her visit."

"But it got more serious…"

"We enjoyed each other's company."

"Were you a daddy figure…or what?"

"More like 'or what'."

"Really? Was it…serious?"

"I didn't let it get that way…just friends."

Erica paused and took a sip of her cocktail before saying, "During that mine collapse…I got the impression she would have given her life for you."

Tom shook his head. "She wanted to help *you* get free of the fallen rocks."

"Yeah, she sure is a gutsy person."

A waiter arrived with their dinner, and Tom was relieved that Erica had something else to hold her attention.

But that didn't last, and Erica was asking about Lisa again.

"She just stopped coming to see you?"

"She hasn't ridden over on her horse since she started classes. She's pretty busy, I imagine. I miss seeing her, sure. I did run into her and her mom at the store. We talked about her school and studies for a couple minutes, but her mom dragged her away…in a nice way."

"Well, there really isn't anywhere that relationship can go. I mean, her being so young and all."

Tom didn't reply but only shrugged. He feared talking himself into a trap.

"I imagine she has guys at college who would die to take her out. Is she dating anyone?"

"I never asked. It really isn't my business."

Her voice softened. "She needs to meet someone her age for any relationship. Don't you think?"

Tom nodded. "Sure. Makes sense. I imagine that's what'll happen."

Tom was hoping Erica would tire of talking about Lisa. She had long been aware of Lisa's crush on Tom and had sometimes voiced disapproval of it. But Tom enjoyed Lisa's company, a beautiful and sexy girl who won Tom's heart.

"You say she's going for a scholarship to the university?"

"Uh-huh. She's a smart girl. I hope she gets on a good vocational track and doesn't waste her life."

"That's kind of out of your control."

"I'll coach her when I get a chance."

"Really? You just can't let go, huh?"

Tom felt irritation but tried to stay calm. "It's not like that. I just want her to head down a good path."

"You're not her dad."

"He's not there for her very much; he drinks a lot. Her mother tries to keep her going straight."

Erica scowled. "That doesn't leave much room in you for anyone else."

Sensing quicksand, Tom tried to deflect what he thought was coming. "I've been busy with the place and getting all the legal stuff done to protect the title and water rights. Not enough hours in the day."

"I'd like it if we could stay friends. I like you."

Tom looked slightly past her. "The events of a year ago brought us closer as friends, and I'd like to keep it going. You're a good person, and I have a lot of respect for you."

It seemed that Erica was fighting to not make a scowl. "Respect…uh-huh…that is important too."

The rest of their meal passed with conversation driven mainly by Tom's questions about her election and work as Sheriff. Erica seemed happy to respond and talk about her duties and expectations.

Tom visited Becky Durance at the Fast Outfitter the next day to thank her for her support and patience. He had been thinking a lot about her recently, particularly remembering the trim, statuesque figure and a face that was easy on the eyes.

Over the past year, Tom had made many trips to the Fast Outfitter as he worked on his cabin, fence, and barn. He parked his truck in the back by the loading dock. This gave him an excellent reason to pay for his goods at the register at the back of the store, usually operated by Becky Durance. They enjoyed conversation with each other and would continue until interrupted by another customer coming to the register. After a few months, a friendship had blossomed. That day, he asked her if she would have a drink and dinner with him when she got off work. She smiled and accepted, asking that they not go to a fancy place as she was not dressed for it, just coming off work.

Tom picked her up at her apartment as she got home. She requested they go to Carlo's Pizza as she had yearned for a pizza for days. The family restaurant was crowded and noisy, but it wasn't long for a booth to become available. As they waited for their food, they spent the time with small talk.

"You said you had gone to Jr. College?"

"I did. My parents couldn't afford to send me to Missoula for a business degree. My mom is a nurse at Harlow Rehab Hospital. My dad is a bookkeeper at the BNSF office."

"They live in Missoula?"

Becky nodded. "My grades were good but not high enough to warrant a scholarship."

"Don't give up. A partial scholarship may be available."

"Yes. I'm hopeful. In the meantime, I'll keep working and saving my money. My dad has an uncle who's up in years and owns a company in Missoula. Dad thinks I could get a job there that pays better than Fast Outfitter."

"Really? What company is that?"

"G&E Packaging. I'm not sure what they do. I guess I should at least interview there."

"I've heard of it. Who owns the company?"

"Well, it's my dad's uncle, Antonio Giordano."

"I think I read something about him."

"Dad said he used to be in the rackets years ago."

Their food arrived, and they attacked the pizza with a ravenous appetite. Conversation was suspended for a few minutes until half the pizza had disappeared.

"What about boyfriends? Nothing serious?" asked Tom.

Becky shook her head. "There've been several." Then she grinned, "None I'd take home to my parents. What about you?"

"Last year was rather a tumultuous year. I worked closely with a woman who is now the Sheriff and a teenage girl who is now in junior college. I haven't had time, what with all the work I do on my place, to make new friends."

"What are you doing nowadays?"

"I bought a horse a while back. That keeps me busy, what with riding him and keeping the barn and corral in good shape."

"Didn't I read that you found the plane that went down near here?"

"Uh-huh. I was helping the Sheriff by doing a search. She didn't have the manpower, and it had to be found quickly."

"But the pilots were dead…"

"They were, and a day later, a gang went in there and scooped up all the cargo and made off with it: a plane load of drugs."

"Wow. No idea where it went? The Sheriff, the FBI…?"

"I haven't heard anything from them. I have my own ideas about it."

"I guess the FBI will come up with something soon. Don't you think?"

Tom shrugged. "I don't know. Hopefully."

A few minutes later, they finished their meal.

"I better get home to bed. I have to be at work early."

Tom put several bills on the table and took a last sip of his drink. Sliding out of the booth, he smiled and helped her put on her sweater.

She looked at him and thanked him. "It was a great pizza. Thanks for coming here."

"Maybe we can do it again?"

"That'd be nice."

It was a short ride to her apartment, and they didn't talk much. When Tom stopped at her place, Becky dug through her purse and retrieved her key.

"I'm glad we're friends."

"Me too," said Tom. "I've wanted to ask you out for some time. I hesitated since I'm a bit older than you."

Becky smiled. "I'm sure glad you finally did. From what I saw at the Outfitter, I've always thought you were a nice guy. So don't be a stranger; you have my phone number."

She kissed him on the lips quickly before she opened her door. She glanced back at him. "Gotta be at work early."

Tom smiled and then watched until she was inside her apartment. "Oh well."

As he drove home, he started to think about Lisa.

Chapter Fourteen
Highland Observer

Rick Sherman stared at his computer screen. Then he rubbed his freshly shaved face and started to compose an article for the Editorial Page on what he knew of the recent plane crash. He wasn't going to leave much out, hoping to jangle someone's nerves to get a clue about the bad actors in this drama. He started with the Camden sheriff being advised last week of a missing plane on its way to Missoula from Seattle. The aircraft had been a non-chartered small-freight carrier without a posted flight plan. It was assumed to have crashed in the bad weather over the mountains from Idaho. Still, its location had been unknown as no locator beacon signal had been received by airplanes or satellites.

He followed by what the Camden sheriff had heard the following night regarding the murder of a DEA agent and his female consort in a motel room. The sheriff had discussed the murders and the missing plane with a friend who volunteered to seek advice on locating the plane from someone experienced in clandestine activities. It seemed to them that the missing plane and the murder of the DEA agent might well be linked.

The sheriff's friend volunteered to search for the downed plane using a sensitive directional radio that hopefully would pick up any weak signal from the aircraft. After studying the terrain on topographical maps, he decided on a probable area to search. After hours on horseback, he located the plane downed in deep timber. He assessed the situation and took many digital photos with his cell phone. It was apparent to him that the crew had perished. Also evident was that the fuselage had burst open on impact and exposed what he surmised was a large amount of packaged cocaine and probably fentanyl. He reported what he had observed to the sheriff. Still, he did not reveal the exact location, holding back that information until he could be assured the area would be policed until the DEA could facilitate the removal of the cargo and the coroner the removal of the bodies.

Days later, after much bureaucratic delay, the FBI and DEA arranged with the National Guard to lower a crew to the crash site by winch in a helicopter to guard the plane and cargo and to retrieve the bodies of the deceased crew members. The plan was to retrieve the cargo using heavy netting to a helicopter. When the FBI arrived on site, they discovered the cargo to be missing. Many tracks of men and horses were observed. Later, the FBI followed the tracks to the McAllister ranch a dozen miles east.

Witnesses at the ranch reported the cargo arrived by horseback and was seen to be put into a white truck. The license plate identified this truck as one owned by the G&E Company.

A letter was received the next day from the editor of the Highland Observer from G&E. The letter was in protest, claiming incorrect statements and that G&E is not involved in any nefarious activity. Also, continuing this libelous action will result in a suit for damages. It was signed by Antonio Giordano, CEO.

Tom stepped out of his cabin the following evening to investigate why the alarm had gone off. He had left his gun inside, confident of a minor incident with a deer. Suddenly, an old reddish Jeep drove rapidly onto the property. He assumed another treasure hunter was inquiring about trespass to search for the plane. The Jeep stopped abruptly in front of the cabin.

Two men immediately jumped out of the vehicle and rushed to attack Tom with clubs. Tom, shocked by the brazen assault, tried to fend off the blows, but they quickly beat him to the ground. They warned him about his involvement with the law in stirring up trouble 'in other people's business.' They left quickly, and Tom didn't see a license plate. He felt foolish for his unguarded moment but then swallowed his pride and called Sheriff Erica with a vague description of the thugs and their vehicle.

Erica came to his cabin in uniform with a young deputy, who made out the report. Tom refused medical help, saying he wanted to go to bed. Tom assumed the trouble had come from G&E and said that to Erica. She shook her head as she left. "I don't expect to find the Jeep any time soon."

Tom, humiliated and very angry, called Rick to vent his rage.

"What the hell? You have no idea who these guys were?"

"Never saw them before. They drove a shitty red Jeep with more rust than paint. I don't remember about the license plate."

"These were white guys or what?"

"Yeah, maybe in their thirties."

"And what, you concluded they were G&E guys?"

"Who the hell else would have done this?"

"Could be some assholes looking for the plane."

"No, I've seen lots of *them*. They drive up and ask stupid questions. That's who I thought these guys were initially."

"And you're pissed. You want to return their greeting?"

"Exactly."

"You're probably right," said Rick. "Those G&E guys may have it in for you. We're talking millions of dollars for that cargo. They damn near lost it all."

"G&E is in the middle of all this," said Tom. "I can't prove it, but I'd be willing to bet they're calling the plays."

"We know the mob owns the company. Maybe they bought the place to do exactly what you're thinking: drug distribution in western Montana."

"We're going to have to put eyes on those creeps; gotta check out the owners and managers."

"Yep. We'll come up with a plan."

"Talk to you later." Tom hung up the phone.

Chapter Fifteen

Plan Developed

Tom and Rick met with Larry the next day to discuss the drug traffic coming in from Seattle. They sat in his office since the lounge was busy at lunch. Dianne had brought in cold beer and a snack tray.

"As I told you before, rumors have it the real owners of G&E are probably mobsters from Seattle or maybe even Chicago."

Tom nodded, "We have to find out who they are…and follow the money."

Rick agreed. "There's got to be a whole organization behind this, maybe centered in Seattle."

Tom scowled. "What's the FBI doing about the two murders here in Camden? A dead DEA agent has got to get their attention even if the state is slow to move."

"You would think so," said Larry. "I talked to the FBI earlier this morning; I've known a guy named Porter for years. He said they had a few agents looking into the murders, but there's nothing to report."

"I asked Erica what the state was doing," said Rick. "She doesn't think it's on top of their list."

"Be that as it may, I've been in contact with some players from back in the day," said Larry. "They've been sending me some interesting information. Porter said he can identify specific players from Mexican cartels that he's linked to the Seattle drug business."

Tom showed some impatience. "How about here in Camden and in Missoula?"

Larry nodded. "Porter said the FBI has had their eye on G&E for some time, ever since new owners took over. However, up to now, their main interest was racketeering and taxes."

"They sound like solid citizens," scowled Tom.

"I called around guys I knew at the bureau," said Larry. "They're sending me IRS and SEC information regarding current G&E management and their financial statements."

"Like what?" said Rick.

"They tell me the sale of G&E occurred two years ago after several years of losses. The sale price was well below market value, and they sold to a group from Seattle headed by Antonio Giordano. He's a well-known mob investor in suspicious businesses."

"Antonio Giordano," said Rick. "I don't know that name."

Larry shrugged and continued. "This business was restructured, keeping it as a packaging company and retaining its previous name. The current financial statement showed a slight increase in profitability at $130M in earnings for the year. No impact of drug transactions was evident in the financial records. They're keeping their books clean."

"Bullshit, we've got to follow the money trail," said Tom. "There always is one."

"Yeah, you're correct," said Larry. "But we have to find a place to start. There's a lot of circumstantial evidence considering the downed plane and the violent reaction by criminal groups. We only *suspect* G&E of being the key distributor of drugs coming into Missoula from Seattle. Let's pry into these things and see if we can't find a place to start so we can unravel this puzzle."

Tom nodded.

Rick asked, "What do we know so far for sure?"

"For sure? Very little. All conjecture," said Tom.

"We know drugs are coming into Missoula airport from Seattle," said Rick. "You can bet your ass distributors are moving the stuff into Camden and every other town around here."

"We know the drugs in the plane ended up in a white truck belonging to G&E," said Larry.

"Yeah," said Tom, "we can reasonably conclude that G&E is operating as a transit point for shipments from Seattle to distribution points in the area."

"Well now," said Larry, rubbing his chin, "this is where it gets fuzzy."

"Yeah, well, I have to wonder if G&E is a mere transit point or are they running the show?" said Tom.

"All associated expenses are off-books as records of these expenses were not found in reported financial statements, according to Porter," said Larry. "So, where exactly are they keeping their records?"

Rick sat up in his chair. "It appears that the standard operating method for G&E regarding the drug business is to receive the drug cargo from a Seattle airplane at Missoula airport, truck it to the G&E facility, and then rapidly repackage and/or ship the cargo to other centers in the area in their trucks preferably within 24 hours or have other parties pick up cargo at G&E. The trucks have to return to G&E quickly to minimize attention and exposure.

Larry shook his head. "I don't know about all that. It's not practical to follow the white trucks to distribution points in the area. It's not worth the effort. The way I see it, the main goal is to *stop* drugs coming from Seattle. We have to catch the big fish, the boss of the operation at G&E." He got up from his chair. "I'll be back in a couple minutes."

Chapter Sixteen

Takedown

Larry came back from the bar with three mugs of cold beer. He picked up where they had left off. "Remember one thing, guys. There is no legal evidence that G&E is involved in the drug business. It is all conjecture. The cops haven't turned up anything."

Tom grabbed a mug and sat back. "I'm sure they're more than just involved."

Rick scowled. "Yeah, without real evidence, we have to tread carefully."

Larry continued, "Once the white truck comes back to G&E from the airport, it seems to me they would want to unload it quickly, and then repackage the drugs, and get that shit out of the building to the distributors. I imagine they would sanitize the area where they repackaged the stuff so if the cops were to bring dogs, they wouldn't detect anything. Anyway, that's what I'm thinking."

Tom shook his head. "To have the distributors from various places in the area arrive at the G&E plant at the appropriate time, the G&E guys would have to know when the plane arrives in Missoula."

"You're right about that," said Rick. "G&E has to do this operation at their plant very fast, or people will get suspicious. I don't think they can afford to have distributors parked out back. That'd be a big red light for the cops."

"Well then, how is the stuff distributed? They can't afford to keep it in the plant, very risky," said Tom.

"Yeah, you're right," said Larry. "G&E will want to operate as a legitimate business and not bring attention to the drug operation. So, they have to get the stuff to the distributors as fast as possible, clear the plant, and clean it."

"They sure can't have distributors showing up randomly at the back of the plant or on a fixed schedule," said Tom. "That'd be surely noticed."

"So, the question is how they alert distributors that a delivery from the airport has been made?" said Rick. "I think they have to get rid of the stuff as quickly as possible, clean the place, and be business-as-usual in a short time or risk discovery."

"Hey guys," said Larry, "suppose they don't distribute at G&E; instead, G&E is just a repackaging stop. They could move the stuff to some other place, some out-of-the-way storage site somewhere, where distribution could be made quietly. What do you think?"

Tom rubbed his chin. "So why go to G&E at all? Just go directly to this warehouse."

Larry spoke. "The drugs probably come packaged in standard quantities, maybe in packs of a kilogram or two. The distributors probably want other quantities. At G&E, they have all the equipment and materials to repackage the stuff to any specific distributor wishes."

"That makes a lot of sense to me," said Rick, looking at Tom, who nodded.

"Listen," said Larry. "On another point, we must identify the bosses and key managers. These guys have to be arrested at the site of some transaction. We can nab the guys at this warehouse, but they'd be only lower-level guys. We must nab the bosses with their hands in the cookie jar."

When Rick was about to speak, Larry raised his hand. "I want to caution about talking to Erica too much about our plans and what we're thinking since whatever the Sheriff's Department decides to do has to be coordinated with the state DCI and, of course, with Missoula."

"I found that out already," said Tom. "The DA's office leaks like a sieve."

"I think we can say," said Rick, "when the white truck arrived from the airport, the contents were moved quickly into the G&E building. *We* don't know how or if the stuff is repackaged there, nor do we know about any storage site where distributors come to get the stuff."

"It seems to me they need to get the stuff *out* of the G&E plant to a warehouse or to distributors quickly; otherwise, they risk discovery," said Tom.

Rick raised a hand. "There's got to be records kept somewhere, maybe on someone's smartphone. You can't run a high-value business without some record-keeping. We need to get our hands on these records."

"Yes indeed," said Larry. "There has to be records of who got what and what payments were made. Nowadays, you can be sure all records are electronic, maybe on cell phones somewhere. It is important that we know who holds these phones so we can trace them and get the data from them or their service providers with a court order."

Tom waved his hands. "Whoa, we're getting way ahead of ourselves. G&E is in Missoula, in a different county. Erica is sheriff of Camden County and has no jurisdiction in Missoula…and we sure as hell don't."

"Shit, he's right," said Rick. "Once the drugs from the plane got into the white truck, it was driven out of this county."

"Damn, I forgot all about that," said Larry. "So, everything we've been discussing is not in our county."

"Yeah, but we can't just forget about it," said Tom. "That shit will be distributed to every damn county around here, including Camden. And let's not forget, there were two murders here in Camden."

"I guess Erica has to work with the police in Missoula in some fashion," said Rick, "but *they* have to do the heavy lifting."

"So, what will we be doing?" said Tom.

"Why don't we find out who is running things at G&E," said Larry. "Let's see what network they've set up for distribution. Is there a warehouse?"

Tom and Rick nodded together.

"You can bet your ass Camden is in this network, as are all the towns around here."

"How do we start?" said Tom.

"Find out who is involved at G&E when the white truck arrives," suggested Larry."

"Okay, I'll drive down to Missoula and hang there for a couple days," said Rick. "I'll keep an eye on the goings on at G&E."

"You can get time off to go there?" said Tom.

Rick shrugged. "A couple days."

Chapter Seventeen
Ambush

Rick had made himself comfortable in his rented car while parked behind G&E Packaging. He was just finishing his coffee when he saw several headlights come on almost at once in the G&E parking lot. A chill went up his back. Had he been discovered?

The vehicles organized and moved in his direction; he knew he'd been discovered. As the lights raced toward him, he realized escape had been cut off. Rick managed a quick panic call to Tom just as several armed men surrounded his vehicle.

Tom had picked up the phone after the first ring.

"Tom, I'm in trouble…"

"Rick? What's happening? You still at G&E?"

"Yeah. Some assholes are going to grab me. They have guns."

"What…?"

A pistol smashed into his side window, and two men wrestled Rick from the car. A guy grabbed Rick's pistol and tossed it back across the seat. The two men, now with the aid of two others, pummeled Rick with their fists, dragged him to one of the cars, and forced him into the back seat with one of his captors. When Rick tried to talk, another fist slammed into his face. Then the car was moving.

The car stopped suddenly, and Rick saw a dilapidated metal storage shed at the edge of the G&E parking area. He was dragged from the car and tied securely to a metal column in the center of the near-empty building. The apparent leader of the men landed a hard blow to Rick's face as they departed from the building, but nothing was said.

Rick struggled to keep calm as the pain overwhelmed him, and blood and saliva flowed off his jaw. Plastic zip ties cut into his wrists and ankles. He struggled to understand why he had been attacked and summarily tied up and left in the storage shed. It seemed to him the goons wanted him away from the G&E buildings, as maybe a drug shipment from the airport would arrive soon. He wondered how long it would be before he was discovered. He realized his cell phone was likely still in his car.

As the first hour ticked by, Rick's pain and anger grew. He knew Tom would be looking for him and likely had others engaged. But Tom was an hour away; would the goons let him live to be found? What had he stumbled onto?

It all made sense to him now. The head of these thugs was probably the new mob-affiliated owner of the G&E plant. Rick figured the owner was running a drug distribution network in Missoula. The two G&E pilots flew the Cessna 210 to Seattle, procured the drug cargo, and flew it back to the Missoula airport. The cargo was loaded into the white truck and delivered to the G&E plant. Rick wasn't sure how the drugs were distributed, but he was sure it had to be done quickly to avoid detection.

Rick struggled to find a position against the metal pole that lessened the pain in his wrists and legs. After a couple hours, he could hardly stand the pain in his ankles and wrists.

Chapter Eighteen

Look for Rick

Tom immediately called Erica at the sheriff's office.

"Sheriff Erica Stewart."

"Erica, this is Tom."

"What's wrong?"

"Rick just got grabbed by some gun-toting goons at G&E and taken somewhere. He was scouting the back of the G&E plant for what he could learn. He said the white truck was missing."

"Damn, *you* let him do that by himself?"

"Yeah. If something unusual happened, he was to call me."

"We must rescue Rick, but first, *you* must find him."

"Since the white truck wasn't there, maybe a shipment arrived at the airport," said Tom.

"Damn it, Tom. Look for Rick! When you find out where he is, call me. I'll ask Missoula to send out some deputies. I've got to get Missoula on board with this. They won't be happy."

"Is the DA down there okay with this operation?"

"No. Why would he be? I'm not asking permission or informing them until after the event concludes. We can't have any leaks right now. It's up to Missoula PD to deal with their DA."

"I hope you can get the police down there to see it your way."

"Yeah. Find Rick and stay in touch."

Tom grabbed his gun and an extra clip and hurried to his truck. He hoped he wouldn't be too late. Missoula was almost 45 minutes away on a good day.

Tom drove directly to the rear of the G&E building. He saw Rick's rental car with the smashed driver's window at the edge of the property. He used his handkerchief to pull open the driver's door to not add to any fingerprints. Tom picked up Rick's cell phone and gun, which lay on the floor. He saw that the last call had been to him and pocketed the phone and gun. There wasn't any clue as to where Rick had been taken. He sat in his pickup, trying to calmly assess the situation, but grew increasingly angry. Had Rick gotten into a deadly situation, he wondered?

He looked toward the loading dock, but the white truck was not there. If there was a delivery tonight, the car from the airport would show up soon, and all the thugs would be busy unloading the cargo at the loading dock. So, Rick had to be somewhere where they could have got back to the loading dock quickly, he thought. If the goons had been pressed for time, they would have had to park Rick somewhere until after the drugs arrived and had been distributed. To Tom, that meant Rick was nearby, somewhere in a five-minute radius, and hopefully still alive.

Convinced of this scenario, Tom drove his truck along the edge of the G&E property. He looked at the many more minor metal storage-type buildings clustered beyond the parking and loading areas and near the property line. He saw that on the front side of the G&E building was a regular street with many other businesses, making it unlikely the goons would have taken Rick in that direction. Behind the G&E plant and parking area, Tom saw acres of scrub brush and saplings growing in a vacant lot. He stopped his pickup there and looked at the back of the G&E building, paying particular attention to the seemingly unoccupied metal buildings that bordered the back of the property. He looked at each metal building for anything unusual. They were boringly similar and untended.

A paper and cardboard recycling plant, Burleson Salvage, was located at the southern end of the G&E property. G&E had several smaller metal buildings at that property line. As Tom looked toward them, an SUV pulled away from one of the buildings and rushed toward the G&E loading dock.

Tom waited until the SUV was at the G&E building, and the men had left the vehicle to go inside. He then drove slowly along the street to approach the group of metal buildings. He parked his pickup on the Burleson Salvage property. He checked his gun and placed it under his belt at his back. He hesitated to use it, considering the nightmare legal issues that would envelop him. But better safe than sorry, he concluded. He strolled from one metal building to another and tried the doorknob of each. He found the door locked at the fourth building, as had been the others. However, in front of the door were what looked like recent scuffs and drag marks that might have been produced by heels dragged over the dusty concrete. He tried the doorknob again, but it was locked. Frustrated, Tom took his fist and slammed it against the door. A loud metallic sound came from inside the building. He thought he heard someone call and wracked his knuckles on the door.

"Hey! Get me outa here!"

"Rick?"

"Get me outa here!"

Chapter Nineteen
Organizing

Erica sat at her desk and pondered the circumstances of the past week. It is apparent, she mused, that Missoula was a central point for incoming drugs and related distribution but out of her area of responsibility. However, drugs coming into Missoula would be distributed to all towns in the western part of the state. Acknowledging this made her keen to stop the drugs coming from Seattle. But how could she get the Missoula officials and state agencies to agree to their responsibility?

She had been told the owners of G&E were gangsters. The plane had been leased by G&E. G&E. had employed the pilots The truck belonged to G&E. She wondered if the transport of drugs from Seattle to G&E in Missoula was solely managed by the gangster owners of G&E, but then who managed the drug distribution to the various sellers at the small towns. Erica concluded that any raid would have to catch the event manager, who could lead them to the bosses at G&E, conspirators at a bare minimum.

But this wasn't her show. Any operation in Missoula had to be by local police officers, not the Camden County sheriff. Erica knew she had little time to convince Missoula of what was happening and hoped they would take up the challenge.

Erica picked up the phone and called David Pritchard, a senior detective in the Missoula Police Department.

"Hello, David. It's Erica again."

"Hi. What's up?"

"Rick was captured at G&E by armed men. He managed a flash phone call to Tom before the call went silent."

"Jeez, what's going on?"

"Tom just left here on his way to Missoula to rescue him. Haven't heard back yet. Don't know if he needs help."

"And what, no one thought to call Missoula PD?"

"David, it just happened…I'm calling."

"Okay…Okay. What do you want me to do?"

"Rick was watching the back of G&E to see what he could learn about drugs being trucked in from the airport. This was his and Tom's theory. He wanted to witness the unloading of the cargo from the plane, see how they dealt with it."

"Erica, I am getting rather upset about guys from Camden coming down here stirring up trouble. I don't need this."

"I was hoping you would want to catch these bad guys red-handed with the goods and take them off the board."

"Just like that? You know how things are done. You can't just pick up the phone and expect me to jump through hoops."

"Dave, I do have a real interest in this. This whole thing started with the murder of a DEA agent and the crash of an airplane *in my area*. I don't want more drugs making their way to Camden or to any other town in the state."

Erica heard Dave sigh. "All right, I'll send a couple detectives out to see what they can make of it. Then, if we have anything, we'll head up an effort to get these drug criminals rounded up. It will be *only* a Missoula PD operation."

"I understand. Please ask the detectives to watch for Tom and Rick."

"All right. Later."

Erica then called Tom's phone, but the call went unanswered. She then called Rick, but no one answered.

Tom retrieved a crowbar from his pickup and worked for a minute before the door sprung open.

"Rick! What the hell…?"

"Get me loose. Let me outa here!"

"Geez, Rick, what the hell happened?"

Tom took his penknife from his pocket and began seeing through the plastic ties. The plastic was difficult to see, and Rick was impatient and angry.

Rick told Tom of being captured and brought to the metal building. "I think the bastards wanted me out of the way while they received the stuff from the white truck."

"Yeah, I just now saw the truck pull in. It was backing to the dock."

"Damn it, I want to break some heads."

"Stay still while I cut through the ties on your ankles."

"I want to get a hold of those bastards, kick some ass."

"It'll be a few more minutes. I'll need to get some first aid stuff from my truck and clean up your ankles and wrists. They're bleeding."

"Later. First, I want to crack some skulls."

"Yeah, yeah, hang on a couple more minutes."

"We have to get out of here before those goons return."

"Almost done…there, you're free."

Rick rubbed his wrists and then his ankles. "I appreciate you're finding me. I really do."

"Yeah, I know you do. Let's get out of this tin can."

Tom reached behind him, pulled the pistol under his belt, and handed it to Rick. "I grabbed this and your phone from your car. They were on the floor."

"Yeah, thanks." He pocketed the phone, removed the clip, looked at it, and pushed it back into the pistol. "I've got nine shots. I hope you have more with you."

"I've got an extra clip in my pocket." Tom looked at Rick and scowled. "I don't plan on starting a war."

Rick nodded. They went to stand behind a metal shed closer to the G&E building and observe the activity at the loading dock. A white G&E truck was being unloaded by four men. Two forklift vehicles were used to quickly take the cargo into the building. The men on the dock were working rapidly. The only light was what was coming through the translucent flexible doors and a bare light bulb over the entrance.

"They're putting the stuff just inside the building," said Tom.

"Yeah, they want to get it done fast. There are two dudes off to the right in the shadow; it looks like they're both on the phone."

"We need to look at the guy running things," said Tom, "find out who he is."

"Hey, it looks like they're done emptying the truck. So now all the shit is inside the building."

"Careful, an SUV just pulled up to the dock," said Tom. They both concentrated their attention on the new arrival. The driver turned the SUV back up to the loading dock. The back door suddenly opened. One of the men on the phone came to stand at the pier where the SUV waited. In less than a minute, a man pushed a dolly loaded with a cardboard box through the flexible doors. It was apparent the box had significant weight, as when the man jumped off the dock to load the box into the SUV, he struggled to handle it. When the back of the SUV was closed, the driver moved away quickly. Just as quickly, another SUV drove to the loading dock and backed up to it.

"Those two guys in the shadows on the dock are coordinating the arrival of the SUVs and the loading. There isn't much light back here," said Rick. "There isn't any traffic on the street either."

"I bet in a couple hours they'll have all of the cargo repackaged and loaded into SUVs and hauled outa here to some storage place."

"Yeah, the two guys on the dock with the phones are orchestrating this operation," said Rick.

"They must keep the SUVs parked elsewhere and call them in as one gets loaded and departs."

"Yeah, smooth operation; do it fast and in the dark."

"So how do we find out who is running this show?" said Tom.

Rick glanced around. "I don't see any cops anywhere. Was Erica going to call Missoula PD?"

"That's what she said. But I don't know this Missoula cop she talks to; he might not go along. Look, I don't want this to become a shoot-out; that'd get us nothing but jail time."

"Okay. So, what do we do? We need to find out who is running this operation," said Rick.

"I think we can safely assume whoever is left in the building tonight is part of this," said Tom. "The regular workers have probably left hours ago."

"I believe that. So, what do we do?"

"Let's copy the license plates of all cars parked around the side and out front. Then let's see if we can get in through the front door; not likely," said Tom. "Or we can capture one of these dudes, take him to that metal shack you were in, and convince him to talk."

"Yeah. We can sneak along the side of the business next door, get plate numbers, and see if the front door is locked. If we get in, we'll have to be very stealthy, or those bastards will shoot us. I'd rather grab one of those guys out here and work him over in the shack."

"Let's go next door and sneak along the boundary and copy plate numbers," said Tom. "Then we can figure out how to grab one of those guys."

"I'd bet those two guys on the dock worked me over in that shack."

It took them ten minutes to copy the license numbers of all the vehicles parked on the side of the building and the two parked in front. They returned to the metal building and watched the coming and going of cars at the loading dock.

"I bet there are two heavyweights in the building right now, and it's their cars out front," said Tom.

"Yeah, I'm sure that's right. How about we grab one of those two goons up on the dock and convince him to talk to us," said Rick. "I'd like a chance to smash one of those guy's faces in."

"I don't think Missoula PD is coming here. Erica probably couldn't convince them to play ball."

"That might make it easier for us…not worrying about them. Let's sneak up close to the right side of the dock where it's dark and lure one of those two guys to us," said Rick.

"Yeah, it's a plan."

Tom and Rick went from one storage shack to another. They hid behind equipment as they made their way up along the edge of the Burleson Salvage property until they got even with the end of the G&E loading dock. They squatted behind a storage bin and watched the two men on the loading dock. The area was dimly lit, and it was in complete darkness near where Tom and Rick were hiding.

Tom whispered to Rick, "We can go over to the dark end of the dock where I will make some suspicious noise so one of those guys comes to check it out. Suppose you huddle at the end of the dock so the guy can't see you. Then, when he steps to the edge of the dock, you reach up and grab his ankles and pull him to the ground."

"Okay. Then what? The other guy will see something is wrong."

"He's not going to abandon the stuff to come see what's going on. We'll do this when he is busy bringing stuff out to load in an SUV," said Tom.

"Yeah. I can't wait to beat the crap out of one of those guys."

Chapter Twenty

Clash at Loading Dock

Tom and Rick positioned themselves in the deep shadow at the far end of the loading dock as a panel truck backed up to the loading area. Following a brief conversation, one of the men on the loading dock entered and came out on a forklift with two boxes. The driver gave the man on the loading dock what looked like a document and then opened the back compartment of the truck and placed the two boxes inside.

Rick looked at Tom and whispered. "The next guy that drives up…as soon as he gets out of his car, we'll distract the guy on the dock. We need him to come over here so I can grab him."

"Te tease him at first. We don't want him to get suspicious and go inside for help."

"Yeah, you're right. We don't want him to think he'll need help."

They didn't have long to wait. A minute after the truck had left the dock area, a car backed into the loading dock.

"These guys have all been here before. They know exactly what to do," said Rick.

"Okay. I'm ready to try and distract the guy coming through the flex curtain."

"Yeah. Let's try."

Rick got into position. Tom uttered a low whistle tone. The man at the loading door stopped and looked towards the dark end of the dock. Then he shook his head and went to the pier's edge just above the car that had backed up there. Tom uttered another low whistle tone. As did the man on the dock, the car driver turned toward the sound. Tom could see the two men exchange comments. The man from the car handed the guy on the pier something, and that man went into the building through the flex doors. He reappeared shortly, driving the forklift with two boxes on the tines.

Tom gave another low whistle. The man stopped the forklift, got off, and listened. The man in the waiting car apparently heard the whistle and watched as the man on the dock strolled toward the dark end of the pier. He seemed not to be alarmed but instead curious as he had not pulled his gun that could be seen under his waist belt. He continued to the end of the loading dock with slow steps while straining to see into the darkness.

The man had stepped to the edge of the loading dock no sooner than Rick reached up, grabbed both ankles, and heaved with all his strength to bring the man down. Tom immediately sat on the man's chest, grabbed the man's gun, and jammed the barrel into the man's mouth. The man gagged and choked with terrified eyes, staring at Tom and Rick.

When Rick heard a car door slam and an engine start, he jumped up to peer around the edge of the loading dock. "Car leaving. Don't see anyone on the dock."

Tom and Rick struggled with the confused and scared man and got him standing. Tom jammed the pistol into the man's ribs while Rick pushed his gun under the man's chin. Tom pushed the man into the yard area of Burleson Salvage and then back toward the metal building where Rick had been held. When the man started to object, Rick slapped the gun barrel on the man's head, "Shut the hell up!"

They hurried towards the metal storage shack. Rick opened the door and pushed the man inside.

"What…what do you guys want?"

Rick picked up remnants of the plastic cable ties that had secured him to the steel pole in the shack's center. He struggled to make two useable ties and fastened the man's wrists to the metal pole. He wasn't sure how long the relationship would hold, but they had to do.

"Why are you doing this? What the hell do you guys want?"

Rick punched the guy in the stomach. "You listening? Paying attention?"

The guy nodded while he winced in discomfort. "Yeah…yeah. What do ya want from me?"

"What's your name asshole?"

"Leo…Leon Cusack. What do you guys want?"

"Leo… who's running the operation over there?"

Leo shook his head.

Rick gave him a decisive backhand blow across the face. "Talk to me, Leo."

"I…I don't know the guy," he gasped.

Rick raised his fist. "Sure you do."

His fist came down hard on the side of Leo's face. The man coughed and spat some blood. "Fuckin' bastards…why you doing this?"

Rick backhanded him across the face. "Answer me, god damn it, before I break your jaw."

"Tony…Capone. He… it's Tony."

"Who does he work for, Leo?"

Leo hesitated to answer.

"I'm going to start breaking things, Leo. Are you ready for that? Now, who does this Tony guy work for?"

"Tony…he takes care of things."

"Who runs the company?"

"It…its Giordano, Antonio Giordano."

"So, who is this Giordano dude?" asked Tom.

"I…I guess he owns the company."

"So, this guy manages the drug business as well?"

Leo shook his head. "No… he's in the main office when he's here. He… he's ancient."

"Talk to me, Leo. Who runs the drug business? Who sets things up…the plane and the pilots? Who does all that?"

"Tony…he does all that. He'll kill me…knows I talked to you."

"Leo…what do *you* do in this business?"

"Who…who are you? What do you want with me?"

"Leo …what is it you do here?"

"I do packaging for commercial clients. Machinery, electronics, and stuff like that."

"Uh-huh. Does that include packaging and selling drugs?"

"When the stuff comes in…I help get it packaged for storage and customers."

"So where is this storage place? I want to know."

"I… I've never been to any… don't know."

"There's more than one?"

"Yeah."

"What you call *customers*… they're really distributors. Isn't that right?"

Leo hesitated. "I don't know about all that. Now let me go."

Rick stepped up close to Leo and grabbed him by the throat. "Listen, you bastard. You're one of the guys that tied me up and worked me over. I remember your stupid face." Rick swung the back of his hand hard across his face. "Answer the god-damn question!"

"I…I don't know much. There's a list of people. They come when Capone calls them."

"So, this Capone guy keeps the records and makes the calls…right?"

Leo nodded. "Yeah. He runs things."

"What's he do here for the regular business?" said Tom.

"He's foreman, assigns the work."

"Who's in the building right now?"

"Me and Bruce doing the packaging. Tony Capone is in his office. No one else is here tonight."

"Bruce, who?"

"Sullivan. Bruce Sullivan"

Tom looked at Rick and jerked his head toward the door. The two went outside and closed the door.

"That's probably all we're gonna get out of this guy," said Tom.

"You're right. Let's get the hell away from here before cops show up."

"What about this guy?"

Rick scowled. "Screw him. Someone will find him, or he'll work himself loose."

"Okay. Let's get our wheels and head home. We're not gonna be able to do much here by ourselves."

"Leo will be screaming to his boss, maybe getting the cops looking for us."

"Yeah, let's get out of here," said Tom.

"What are you going to say to Erica? She might blow a fuse."

"I came down to Missoula to look for you. I saw your vehicle parked near G&E, and the window broke out. I walked around until I found you trussed up in a metal shack. I cut you loose. Rick was all pissed off, but since there wasn't anyone around at the G&E place, we just left and came back home."

Rick nodded. "That's the story?"

"Yep. That's the story."

Chapter Twenty One

Culprits

It was 8am when Erica placed her coffee and muffin on her desk and reached for her ringing phone.

"Good morning. Sheriff Stewart."

"Erica, this is David Pritchard. Sorry to bother you so early, but I had a very distressing call last night."

"I haven't had a chance to check the feed. What happened?"

"Yesterday, you asked me to have my officers watch for your two rambunctious friends that went missing here in Missoula. Did you hear from them?"

"I had a short call from Tom last night. He said he had found Rick, and they were coming home. I haven't heard from them this morning."

"Like I said I would, I sent a patrol out last night to look for your two friends. They didn't find them and didn't run across the vehicle you mentioned. However, they walked around G&E and came across a fellow tied up in a storage shack, and it wasn't your friend."

"Tom didn't say much when he called from the road. Only said he had found Rick and were on their way home."

"Very interesting. This guy claims two guys grabbed him at G&E while he was working on the loading dock and dragged him into a shack nearby where they worked him over."

"Wow. What did he have to say?"

"Well, that's the odd part. They kept beating on him, wanting to know who worked at the company. Now, Erica, I ask you…does this sound like a couple of your guys?"

"Damn, David, I can't believe it is. No, it sure doesn't sound like Tom and Rick."

"Well, I got to tell you; we're talking about an arrest warrant for a felony here when I get them identified."

"It sounds so bizarre."

"You have a good day now," said David.

"Yeah, you too."

Tom saw a text message on his cell phone when he woke up. Since it was from Erica, he suspected she had been talking to Missoula this morning. Her message had requested that he come to her office immediately. He quickly called Rick to tell him of Erica's phone message and left for town.

He arrived at the Sheriff's Office at 9:15, and the dispatch operator said he was expected. At Erica's office, he tapped on the door.

"Tom, come in and close the door."

He stood in front of her desk. "I got your text message when I woke up."

"Uh-huh. Pour yourself a coffee if you want."

"Yeah, thanks."

Tom was getting increasingly nervous. This was an odd meeting, he thought. He took a seat in front of her desk.

"Last I heard from you was that you had found Rick, and you both were on your way home."

Tom sipped his coffee and put the mug on the edge of her desk. "That's what happened. We drove both vehicles home even though Rick had his driver's window broken out."

"Good thing it wasn't cold last night. So, you got down there and located him in a storage shed? How'd that happen?"

"When I got there, behind G&E, I parked and watched the area to get my bearings. While looking over the place, I spotted an SUV start-up by one of the metal storage shacks and quickly parked by the loading dock. Something told me to check that place first. I heard him inside but couldn't get the door open. I had to get a crowbar from my truck and pry the door open. They had Rick tied up to a metal pole. He had lots of bruises and bloody wrists and ankles from the plastic ties. He sure was pissed."

Erica sat back in her chair and stared at him briefly. "I expect you to tell me the truth. Either the truth or you decline to answer me. Understood?"

"Yes, of course."

"Anything you want to change so far?"

He shook his head. "No."

"Now, after you freed Rick from the storage shed and before you drove home, what happened?"

Tom squirmed in his seat and drank some of the coffee. "We got to watch what was happening at the loading dock. Every few minutes, an SUV or a car would drive in and back up to the dock. The dock was dark, with only a light over the freight door. The driver would get out, go to the dock, and hand the guy something. Then the guy went inside and came out on a forklift with a box or two on the skids. He would hand the boxes down to the driver, load them in the vehicle, and then be gone. That was repeated several times while we watched."

"Where were you guys doing this watching?"

"We, uh, hiding on the dark side of the loading dock, on the ground."

"What were you guys expecting to learn or see?"

"We hoped to see who was managing the operation."

"Did you?"

He shook his head. "No."

"What happened then?"

Tom was silent and reached for his coffee. He sipped some and put the mug back down. "I don't want to talk about that."

"Well, let me tell you what I heard."

Tom sat back, worried about what was to come.

Erica cleared her throat. "This morning, I received a call from Detective Dave Pritchard of Missoula PD. Earlier, I had asked him to have someone look around the G&E area as I hadn't heard from you and that you had gone there to look for Rick, who you suspected was in trouble."

Tom nodded, and she continued.

"A two-man patrol walked around the neighborhood and eventually came across some guy tied up in a metal storage shack. You follow me so far?"

Tom nodded again. "Yep."

"Has a familiar ring to it, doesn't it?"

Tom shrugged.

"This guy complained to the patrol officers that two men had grabbed him at the loading dock and forced him into the shed and then beat him trying to get him to say who the people were running the operation."

Erica stared at Tom. "Does this seem familiar to you?"

Tom shook his head and shrugged.

"No comment?"

"No."

"Detective Pritchard is convinced you and Rick were the culprits and is considering getting an arrest warrant. If the man in the shed can identify you, I imagine it won't go well for you."

Tom stood up. "Thanks for the information."

"Get the hell out of here."

Chapter Twenty Two
Things Not Going Well

Tom picked up the phone. "Hello."

"Hey, it's Rick. I think we'd better get our heads together. Last night didn't go well, and I think we will both hear about it."

"I already did. She met with Erica a little bit ago. She got a call from her cop friend in Missoula, who threatened to have us identified and arrested. She wasn't happy with me. Let's meet up at Joey's Diner in an hour."

"All right. See ya."

Tom saw Rick arrive, and he waved to him as he entered the diner.

"Hey, your order yet?"

Tom shook his head and signaled the waitress.

"Just coffee and a Danish for me," said Rick.

"Coffee, please, and a stack of rye toast," said Tom. As the waitress walked away, Tom looked at Rick. "I didn't admit to anything other than I went down there to look for you and that I found you trussed up in a storage shed. I told her you had been beaten up by two goons who I then saw drive up to the G&E loading dock."

"You didn't say anything about the dude we worked over?"

"No. I refused to answer her questions about that. Of course, she could assume whatever she wished. The detective from Missoula was hot under the collar about the dude they found in the storage shed. Still, the detective knew nothing about two G&E goons kidnapping you from your car and working you over in one of the storage shacks. She didn't go into that."

Rick shook his head. "We didn't learn much last night. Giordano owns the place, but this Tony Capone guy runs things, including the drug operation, as best we can tell. Leon Cusack and Bruce Sullivan worked there last night, but others might have been there."

"Neither Erica nor the detective in Missoula are very keen on hearing about the drug operation," said Tom. "The plane being found, and the load being stolen is old news. It's going to take solid proof of G&E and drugs before they stick their necks out."

The waitress returned with their order. Rick took a long sip of his coffee and looked at Tom. "What are we expected to do, just forget about this drug thing?"

"The Missoula PD and our sheriff don't seem too anxious to pursue this," said Tom. "If anything, they're probably antagonistic to the very thought of it."

"Should we just forget about it? Let the creeps keep moving and selling drugs in our towns here in western Montana?"

Tom shook his head. "We need to positively tie the G&E guys to the drugs coming in from Seattle. We know it's their plane and their pilots. That's in the public record."

"It's going to take having the law actually catch these guys with the drugs," said Rick, "either at the plane or the G&E building. For that to happen, the police must have a formal complaint with some real proof."

Tom nodded. "I wouldn't be surprised if those guys move their operation now that we caused trouble for them last night. We need to find out where they store their stuff if it's not at G&E. Maybe we do some snooping. Maybe follow the white truck several times and see where they go with the stuff."

"Yeah, that's an idea," said Rick. "We could take turns and not let them catch us at it."

"If we can do this and be able to associate some of those guys with the drugs, it'd be a way to get the police to take it seriously. Maybe get some photos."

"Let's see what we can come up with. My schedule is pretty flexible at the paper. If I tell the boss I'm trying to get a scoop, he'll be more agreeable with my absences."

"I hope we can do more than nail a few low-level guys with drugs. To make a dent in this operation, we need the cops to get the bosses together with the goods."

"We need to know when the plane is coming from Seattle. I'm not sure it happens on a fixed schedule," said Rick.

"I'll revisit Larry and see what he thinks about when the plane enters Missoula. I'm sure he knows how to figure it out."

Rick grinned. "He is one resourceful guy."

"We're not exactly welcome in Missoula," said Tom. "This may get a little tricky."

Rick scowled and nodded. "I don't want to be stopped for a traffic ticket."

"Me neither."

Chapter Twenty Three
The G&E Company

"Hey Tom, you're early. The roast beef isn't done yet."

"Larry, I just came by to run something by you. You have a few minutes?"

"Sure. Come into the office." He signaled to Diane to bring two mugs of cold beer.

In his office, he pointed to the conference table. "Here, have a seat. We'll have a cold one while we talk."

"Larry, let me bring you up to date."

Diane knocked and entered with two frosty mugs of beer and a bowl of pretzels.

"Thanks, Diane. That'll hold us," said Larry as he turned to Tom. "Alright, lay it out for me."

Tom described what had happened the previous days. Larry shook his head as Tom explained what he and Rick had been doing at G&E.

"I think we might get ourselves arrested," said Tom.

"Maybe. Meanwhile, I've been scouring the public records about G&E Company. The company is privately held, and the owner is Antonio Giordano. He's a mobster from Chicago, but he's now 84 years old and not in excellent health. I'm not sure how much he's involved in at the company. The day-to-day running of the place must be the responsibility of this Tony Capone you mentioned. The Thomas Register doesn't list his name, only that of Giordano.

"There's got to be a vice president or second in command. Right?"

"Oddly, there isn't a President listed. Not even a Vice President. However, there is an Associate Vice President listed. His name is James Giordano. Turns out he's a young guy still in college. He's the son of Antonio."

"Wow. Antonio must be pretty spry for his age."

"News articles suggest he is not well," said Larry. "It looks like his son is prepping to step into his father's shoes soon. The old man probably hopes the kid can take over the company."

"Well, if the old man can't keep a grip on these guys, maybe Tony Capone is the real force to be reckoned with," said Tom.

"Yeah, I wonder if the old man even knows what this Tony guy is up to, or if he does, does he have real control of Tony," said Larry.

"I sure would like to know who we're dealing with."

"The old man has a nice old house near the university. It's grouped in with a lot of old mansions. These are very nice places. I doubt there is any criminal activity there. I discovered that this Tony guy has a multi-acre place past the airport. According to the word I got from a friend who lives in Missoula, he's keeping some horses there. He drove by there earlier. There are two barns on the property."

"Well, we don't know," said Tom, "if what we did at the G&E loading dock the other night has caused Tony to rethink where he does his drug business. But a secure second place might be on Tony's estate, especially with the two barns."

"My friend mentioned the estate has many large trees, which could give him cover," said Larry. "I asked him to get me an overhead view showing the nearby roads. That'll take a day or two; he's got to set up his drone."

Tom nodded. "That'd be a great thing to have."

"I'll get it. This guy is good. I'll tell you what, I'll ask him to keep an eye on the back of G&E, and let's see if they move their operation elsewhere."

"We've got to be smarter about what we do."

Larry grinned and nodded. "Yeah, we don't want a repeat of your last performance."

"Let's say we find where they stash and distribute the stuff; what's the next step?"

"Somehow, we have to get proof, like pictures, of the people involved."

"Then we can build a case and convince the Missoula PD?"

"Well, maybe, unless they are in on it too," said Larry with a grin.

"We could take the information to the DEA directly. There's an office in Missoula."

Larry nodded. "That's an idea…best one you've had so far. You go back and talk to Rick to see if he agrees with our statement. Then we'll go to the next step."

"Which is what?"

"Proof. Evidence. That's the job for you two."

Tom stood up. "I'll talk to Rick."

Tom started the coffee maker and then phoned Rick. "Hey, I thought you'd be at the paper; it's almost two."

"I called and checked in. I'm working on an assignment here at home."

"I wanted to tell you I went to see Larry earlier."

Rick chuckled. "Did he call us the Keystone Cops?"

"Not directly. He wasn't too impressed with us, however."

"I'm not too impressed with us either. So, what did he say?"

"I gave him the whole story of the other night. He kept shaking his head."

"It was kind of embarrassing."

"Yeah, well then we got onto how we might more intelligently go about things."

"Did you take notes?"

"Oh hell, I can remember what he said."

"Okay."

"Larry thinks that since we made trouble in the back of G&E the other night, those guys may move their operation to a more secure place."

"Possibly."

"We must find out where they are stashing their stuff and get photo evidence linking it to actual people. That's not so easily done as you can imagine."

"You got that right."

"Larry thinks we may have burned our bridges with the Missoula PD, and when we get the real evidence, we may be better off working with the DEA. They have an office in Missoula."

"I agree with him. The Missoula PD is a lost cause, at least for now."

"Larry said it's up to us, you and me, to get the proof we need to convince the DEA that we have a serious cause worthy of their time and effort."

"Okay. Where do we start? Do we check out this Tony guy first?"

"Yes. Larry thinks that Antonio is too old and ailing, and Tony is likely the real boss at G&E. So, let's look at Tony first."

"Alright, keep in touch. I'll find out Tony's address."

"Okay," said Tom. "See you later."

The phone was ringing as Tom entered his cabin. "Hello."

"Tom, it's Erica; I've called several times."

"Sorry. I was cleaning the stall in the barn and raking up the corral."

Erica sounded annoyed. "You take your cell phone with you?"

"Sometimes."

"It'd be nice if you did."

Her tone of voice didn't sit well with him. "What's up, or don't I dare ask?"

"Detective Dave Pritchard of Missoula PD returned my call this morning, giving me an update. He had a detective scouting at G&E for the last couple of days. He had another detective checking the arrivals at the airport. However, there have been no suspicious arrivals in the last few days, and things at G&E seem normal. Pritchard then arranged with service personnel at the airport fueling station to alert him of any suspicious arrivals, tiny planes like the Cessna 210."

"Okay. What's he going to do now?"

"Pritchard? I don't know. He didn't say."

"I was talking with Larry and Rick. We all agree that the guys at G&E who are running this drug scheme may well change the location for doing the drug distribution since the stew the other night."

"That's possible, sure. What are you guys going to do? Hopefully, stay out of trouble."

"I don't know what we can do at this point. Maybe lay low for a while."

"That would probably be a good idea. Maybe some of your troubles will blow over."

"Okay. Thanks. Gotta go."

Chapter Twenty Four
Tony's Place

It was dusk in Missoula as Tom drove slowly along Newhouse Road. The elaborate multi-acre estate that belonged to Tony Capone was set back on his right several hundred yards from the road. Tom saw a classy two-story ranch house, two barns, and a separate three-car garage suitable for larger vehicles. He thought of how fitting the estate could be as a storage and distribution location. He didn't see horses in the field and wondered if any were in the barn. At the end of the property, Tom turned right onto a smaller but paved street running along the southern border. He was almost out of sight of the house when he saw several horses at the west edge of the estate. He drove along the property's western edge and saw only a vast expanse of grass until he reached the northern border and turned right there. Approaching the buildings from the back, he first passed the two large barns and then the oversized garage closest to the majestic house. Yes, thought Tom, Tony had done well for himself.

Tom drove on and turned into a shopping area where the land was higher than Tony's place. He parked his pickup at the edge of the parking lot facing west and retrieved binoculars from the glove box. They offered a clear view of the estate. Tom tore out a page from his notebook full of shopping lists and drew what he saw of the estate. Only one driveway into the estate went by the luxurious house and onto the two barns. The driveway was wide, easily accommodating a commercial truck. There was a side entrance to the house at the driveway and a primary entryway at the front with a stone path to the driveway. The multi-car garage was opposite the side entry of the house across the driveway. In front of one of the garage doors was parked what looked to Tom as a late model gray Nissan. The two barns seemed overly large, thought Tom, as he had seen only three horses at the far end of the pasture.

Suddenly a large SUV drove up the driveway and stopped at the side entrance to the house. A man wearing a business suit left the vehicle and entered the house. It was too far to read the license plate, but the car seemed like a Chevy Tahoe. He wondered if Tony was just getting home from G&E. He made some notes along the edge of the map he had drawn. He didn't see anyone else, and he wondered if Tony was married with a family. Then, a short woman left the house by the side entrance and walked to the gray car. She drove out to the street and headed north and out of sight.

It was a half hour before Tom saw anyone move in the yard. A man dressed in casual clothes left the house by the side entrance and went to the closest barn, entering by a small door on the visible side. A few minutes later, a tiny SUV drove onto the driveway and up to the barn. At this time the barn door swung open, and the SUV backed in part way. After five minutes, the vehicle came out of the barn, drove down the driveway, and disappeared on the road toward the north.

Tom noticed it was getting dark and realized he should not stay longer and risk a suspicious neighbor calling the police. A meeting with the Missoula Police might not go well, he thought as he started the engine. As he backed out of the parking spot a movement caught his attention. He stopped, stared at the Capone estate, and then coasted back to his parking spot. He picked up his binoculars and turned off the engine. He could see it clearly now, a white panel truck moving slowly up the driveway. When abreast of the first barn, the car stopped, turned, and returned to the barn door, which was still open. The back of the car was hidden from view as it was now inside the barn by a few feet. The driver, a medium sized man with black hair, came out of the cab and disappeared into the barn. He saw no activity on the property for almost twenty minutes. When Tom was about to give up and head for home, the driver appeared and got in the truck cab. A minute later, the truck headed down the driveway, and a man was seen closing the barn doors. The car turned north on the road, and the man at the barn walked back to his house. This is certainly interesting, Tom thought.

Tom picked up his buzzing phone as he headed west out of town. "Hey, Rick?"

"Yeah. Where are you? Not in jail, I hope."

"Just leaving town and headed home. I'll be an hour or so."

"Where in Missoula? You didn't run into the police down there? Erica said they were probably looking for you and me."

"I came down here to check on this Tony Capone guy. I wanted to see what kind of place he had. So, I found a perch on a slope above his estate and watched it for over an hour."

"Estate? The guy has an estate?"

"Oh yeah. It's a really nice setup. I saw lots of fenced acres with three horses. He has a grand house; two stories of stone and brick."

"No kidding? The guy must be doing okay at G&E."

"Indeed. There is a multi-vehicle garage and two big barns. I can see where maybe horses are kept in one, but I am really curious about the other."

"Why's that? Did you see something?"

Tom told Rick what he had seen.

"This is getting interesting. Did you take pictures?"

"I took a few but I was too far away. I sketched a map of the place."

"Let's talk about it when you get back. I can meet you at your place."

"Okay. I'll be there in an hour or so. See you then."

Tom handed Rick a cold beer and sat down at the kitchen table.

"Damn it, Tom, no one gives a shit about this drug business."

Tom shook his head. "I don't think it's that. It's more like everyone is up to their asses in their little lives doing whatever to make a living and not wanting to entertain anymore crap."

Rick scowled. "Well that pretty well sums it up. But you're not the freakin' Lone Ranger and I'm sure as hell not Tonto, so what's the plan?"

"Like I said, the Missoula PD is probably going full out on what they normally have to deal with. They will act on a sure thing, but they're not likely to want to spend resources on our whim."

"So, we have to hand it to them on a silver platter? That's what you're saying?"

Tom nodded, "Right now, it looks like that."

"Oh, for shit's sake, we're here in Camden. The bad guys are in Missoula. How do we work this?"

Tom grimaced, "Remember, here in Camden we still have a dead DEA Agent and so far, no one has been arrested for it. This may only be a side issue, but it should keep Sheriff Erica involved."

"Okay. I'm listening."

"I'm thinking the killer has to be someone in the G&E outfit. I'd like to know who."

Rick nodded. "Yeah, that'd link Camden and Missoula in this drug issue. It may give us a little bit more leverage when it comes to taking names and kickin' ass."

"So, how do we find out who killed the DEA agent?"

"Let's start by getting a list of all the G&E employees. We think it's one of them, so let's find out who," said Rick.

"I'll call Larry. I bet he can get a list from some records somewhere."

"Damn, there's a whole list of questions we have to dig into," said Rick. "For instance, where are the funds coming from to finance the drug buy from Seattle. There's got to be a record of this somewhere."

"Maybe it's all done with cash."

"Could be, but there has to be a paper trail."

"Or it might be all recorded on cell phones," said Tom.

Rick nodded, "They're probably using burner phones."

"Well hell, isn't the FBI supposed to be investigating all this?"

"Are they? Really?"

Tom called Larry later that day.

"You want a list of all the employees? Asking those kinds of questions could get one in trouble."

"You don't think you can get that?" asked Tom.

"Why do you want this information? Trying to get yourself in more trouble?"

"Rick and I want to see who the most likely guys are at G&E that could have killed the DEA agent."

"At G&E? You're certain of that?"

"No, not certain. But we both think it is likely. I suppose it could be a hired hit."

"I have to agree with you based on what we talked about before; a local bad guy at G&E seems probable. Understand this, though; if you go accusing some guy of this shooting, they'll come after you with a vengeance. They won't let you get them identified and arrested. You and Rick may end up dead as well."

"Damn it, Larry, what choice is there?"

"What is your objective here? I thought you were most interested in stopping drugs from entering our towns."

"It doesn't look like the Missoula PD or the DEA or anyone else is taking this drug infiltration from Seattle seriously. Our sheriff in Camden has no real authority in Missoula. If we start to poke around in Missoula again, the cops there won't look at us too friendly."

"That's for damn sure…after your last stunt."

"The only link in Camden to these drug guys is the murder of the DEA agent."

"I'll get the information you want," said Larry shaking his head, "but I'm not going to be responsible for you and Rick being killed."

Chapter Twenty Five

Conjecture

When Tom got home, he found a notice taped to the door. It advised him to leave well enough alone, or the cost would be severe. A picture was printed on the paper above the G&E loading dock door. Tom realized the bright light had shielded the camera from his view. Although somewhat blurry, it was possible to ascertain that the person in the image was Tom. No picture of Rick was evident. He called Rick and described what he had found.

"Damn it Tom, the risk here is real. Remember what Larry warned us. We might be getting in way over our heads. If we get in trouble, the sheriff won't likely be able to help us. I want to help you with this, but keep in mind what Larry said."

"Rick, I hear what you're saying. Ordinarily, I would forget about this. But two people died in Camden, and deadly drugs are coming into our corner of the state. And it seems to me that no one is very interested."

"How about you run this by Erica? Get her opinion on this, just her opinion."

"Okay, I'll call her."

Erica expressed alarm at what Tom was proposing.

"Tom, this is not right. You do not have any evidence to support what you're suggesting. Sure, what you say makes some sense, but it is all conjecture. You're going to get in trouble with the law if you push this; and worse if the guys you roust are indeed killers. I would rather all information and clues be routed to me. I could see that Missoula PD takes action as appropriate."

"Rick is getting a little squishy about this. I know it makes sense to let it go; but what about the two people that were killed, and what about the plane load of drugs coming into our part of the state? Life just goes on?"

Tom heard her sigh. "I don't have the resources to really investigate this. I know some of the drugs ending up in Missoula will certainly find their way back here to Camden, and I will have to deal with that. However, Missoula must be the one to investigate and arrest any bad actors, be they at G&E or elsewhere. I can make suggestions to the PD there, but it's all their call."

"What have you learned from conversations with the Missoula PD, FBI, or the TSA?"

"I keep in touch with them and with DCI, of course. But up until a couple days ago, no useful evidence has surfaced at the scene of the DEA agent murder. DCI obtained video from a camera at the motel office. It showed a white man easily opening the door and going into the room of the DEA agent and then leaving less than a minute later. The camera was too far away from the motel room to capture detail of the person."

"Killer had a key card?," asked Tom.

"Don't know. They suspect the shooter came and went from the truck stop next door as that is the direction the shooter left in the image. Video at the truck stop showed the shooter arrived and left at 11:43pm in a gray mid-sized sedan that was parked at the edge of the truck stop property. Another camera on the truck stop building showed the car as a late model Nissan. The details of the shooter getting into the car were not clear enough for identification. The license plate of the car was not readable. The images from outside the truck stop building indicate that the shooter came and went from the Nissan car without going into the truck stop building. The FBI claimed to still be processing the video from the cameras to try enhancing the images."

"That's it?"

"That's all we have."

"I just wonder why the killer of the DEA agent and his accomplice haven't been identified by now," said Tom. "Was there any street talk about the killing of the agent?"

"Nothing we heard. I think you and Rick should back away and let the FBI do their investigation. I expect the FBI to have an arrest or a suspect soon. Your and Rick's involvement would only complicate things and get you in trouble with the FBI."

"Thanks. I hear you. Let me run this by Rick."

The next day Larry made a list of G&E employees and their past arrests gleaned from electronic intrusion of employer records. He e-mailed the information to Tom, who then met Rick at Joey's Diner for dinner and to discuss the G&E list.

"So, what's good for dinner?" asked Rick.

"It's not bad here for diner food. I will have the Salisbury steak and a slice of pie for dessert."

Rick looked through the menu and then said, "I'll try the steak tips."

"I've had them a couple times. They do a good job here."

After the waitress took their order and left them with coffee, Rick asked, "Let's review the list Larry gave you."

Tom pulled the folded paper from his back pocket and flattened it on the table. "There are twenty-eight names here in no special order. The arrest history, where applicable, is typed in alongside the name."

"Wow. How did he get all this info?"

Tom shook his head. "I didn't ask."

"You looked at this list. What do you think?"

"Nineteen of the names have an arrest record. Three names are of interest to me. Let's see what you come up with."

Rick studied the list and sipped his coffee. He didn't say anything until the waitress arrived with their meals. He set the paper aside and shook his head. "Although nineteen have arrest records, I'd be willing to bet the rest are not choir boys."

Tom smiled, "You have an opinion?"

"Not yet. Have to get after these steak tips."

There was a pause as both attacked their dinner. "How are the tips? You're going right after them."

Rick nodded. "Tender, tasty too."

"Yeah, this place is not highbrow, but the food is good, and it is reasonable. They make some good pies too."

When the waitress came by, they each ordered a slice of pie and more coffee. Rick looked at the list of names and then turned to Tom.

"There are several names that have been in prison. Most have been arrested for something but never went to trial. Most of them came here from the Chicago area. Now that's an interesting group of employees, wouldn't you say?"

"Interesting? Yes."

Their pie and coffee arrived, and they were again silent. Finally, Tom looked at Rick. "Who do you think is our shooter?"

"One or two of these guys could pull it off cleanly. However, if it was me calling the shots, I'd be worried someone would talk or let slip about the hit. Then the cops would be looking at me real closely. Not a good thing."

"What then?" asked Tom.

"Well, if it was me, I'd be inclined to do the deed myself and have no one else know about it. Otherwise, I'd be wondering if someone would sell me out."

"So, who is the shooter?"

"I'm going with Tony, baby. Tony Capone. What about you?"

Tom nodded several times. "I agree with you. It would be too risky for Tony to have someone else do it."

"It's going to be hard to prove."

"I'm thinking we might not have to," said Tom.

"Okay." Rick picked up his coffee cup and took a sip.

"I admit I haven't thought this all out yet. I wonder how we can get Tony to incriminate himself. We need to find a way."

"Whatever we do may have to be here in Camden," said Rick, "since we are persona non grata in Missoula."

"Uh-huh. Need to do something that would bring Tony into Camden."

"The DEA agent's body has been claimed and is long gone. The prostitute's body may still be at the coroners. We don't have much to draw on," said Rick.

"How about the truck stop? Any witnesses? Any camera footage we haven't seen yet?"

Rick nodded. "That is something we have to check. Do you know anybody there?"

"Don't think so. But I'll work on it."

"In the meantime, I must write another item for the op-ed page. Get things stirred up."

Tom grimaced. "I worry what may happen if you poke a stick in their eye. These guys are serious criminals."

Chapter Twenty Six

Stick in the Eye

That evening, Rick posted another article to the op-ed section of the Highland Observer and sent an e-mail copy to the op-ed desk of the Missoula News, thinking that at least one of the G&E culprits would read it. He knew the paper would be on the street late the following day. Although a little nervous, he hoped to get a reaction among those responsible for the murder of the DEA agent. The posted article read:

Murderer Still at Large

It has been several weeks since a DEA agent and his consort were murdered in a motel adjacent to the Camden Truck Stop. To many, it does not stretch credulity to link the murders to the crash of a drug-laden plane in the nearby mountains during the storm. Also, it does not seem to stretch the imagination to think the DEA agent, known to have been from Missoula, to be in Camden following up on the missing plane coming from Seattle destined for Missoula. The video camera witness has provided a description of the killer as being a middle-aged white male who parked a newer model Nissan on the edge of the Camden Truck Stop and walked to the adjacent motel. The license plate was not readable. A video camera at the motel office captured the man arriving on the property from the truck stop and proceeding to the room occupied by the DEA Agent and his consort. Less than a minute later, this person is seen on video leaving the room, walking back to his car at the edge of the truck stop, and driving away.

Currently, the FBI has not yet identified the murderer. Presuming the destination of the cargo plane was Missoula, it seems more than probable that the near-new gray Nissan originated in Missoula, traveled to Camden, and then returned to Missoula. Granted, there are many gray Nissan's in Missoula. Is it likely that one of them is the vehicle in the video, or is this too much of a stretch?

Rick worked late the following day. As the day slid into darkness, he heard what sounded like glass breaking. He went to the window that overlooked the street. A car had stopped alongside his rented sedan. Then, before he could comprehend what was happening, a man smashed his rental car window with what looked like a crowbar, and as he got back into his car, threw a lighted Molotov cocktail into the rental. Rick's mind reeled. Then, in a sudden burst of energy, he ran to the staircase and sprinted down to the first floor. He charged through the front doors only to see the taillights down the street.

As he looked toward his car, the interior exploded in a flame. Fumbling for his phone, Rick called 911, yelled, "Car fire!" and gave his address. Several anxious minutes later, a fire engine and police car stopped behind his burning vehicle. By then, it was a total loss.

The police officer asked for details, but Rick had nothing besides what he'd seen from the upstairs window. Rick didn't think there were cameras except at the back of the building at the loading dock. The officer shook his head and went to his car to make a report. Rick cursed to himself and went back into the building.

At his desk, he left a message for the car rental agency. Then he called Tom and discussed the fire-bombed car and the likely culprit. They both agreed the culprit was someone from the G&E crowd. Who else could it be? They agreed the severity of the violence against them is what one would expect from drug dealers or mob guys.

The following day, Rick was at his desk by 8:30. A few minutes later, the phone rang. He picked it up.

It was a calm voice. "What did you think would happen?"

Rick replied. "Is that your Nissan showing up on video at the truck stop in Camden the other week and at the fire last night? Was that you walking over to the motel from the truck stop?"

The calm voice said, "Do you have some kind of a death wish?"

The phone then disconnected. Rick could not reconnect and was told by a recording, "The phone is no longer in service."

In late afternoon Rick called Tom. "Hey, what are you doing for dinner?"

"Hadn't thought about it. Want to meet at the diner?"

"Yeah, the diner is fine. Good place to talk."

"Okay. Meet you there at 6:30?"

"Sure. I'll be there."

They ordered their dinner and sat back with coffee while they waited.

"I got a call from some goon. He didn't identify himself; he just gave me a warning."

Tom looked at Rick in surprise. "He…someone called you? What did he say?"

Rick shrugged. "Wanted to know if I had a death wish."

"I was afraid of that. They now know what we know," said Tom. "They must assume we're going to ruin their business. They won't put up with that. Things could get even more serious."

"It's probably best if we don't stand around and wait for someone to make trouble. We need to be ahead of them."

"What the hell can we do?" said Tom. "We can't be going down to Missoula and raising hell. That'll surely get us arrested without accomplishing anything."

Rick nodded slowly. "You're right."

"We can't kid ourselves; these guys are gangsters. When we get between them and their source of drugs and money, we could end up dead."

"Uh-huh. We need to get ahead of them and stay ahead of them."

"I think the guys running things will start using different airports in the Seattle area as well as here in the Missoula, keeping us guessing and keeping up their product deliveries."

"You know about these smaller airfields?" asked Rick.

"I looked into it the other day. Four small airfields in the Missoula area are basically daylight-only operations and do not have a control tower. If the mob guys greased the right people, arrangements could be made at one or all of them."

"Have you talked to Erica?"

"Not recently." Tom pulled his phone from his pocket. "Let me check in with her."

He pressed the button on the quick dial.

"Hello, Erica. I'm here with Rick and on speakerphone."

"Hi Tom, you too, Rick."

"Hi. Yes. We were here having dinner at the diner. I wondered what you may have heard lately from the FBI or somebody. For instance, have you listened to who in Seattle paid the pilots to ship the drug cargo to Missoula?"

"Apparently, the FBI arrested two men last week at Seattle loading a plane with drugs. Their destination was Missoula. They both claimed they were paid in cash by the truck driver who brought the cargo. It seems that it is never the same driver or the same truck. The airplane is brought to the airport by other pilots that the two men couldn't identify. The FBI confiscated the plane and cargo, and the men were arrested. I haven't heard anything since. By the way, what kind of trouble are you getting into? I heard about Rick's car going up in smoke. No witnesses, apparently."

"It was a reaction to what Rick wrote in the Op-Ed page the other day."

"I sure hope you two know what you're doing."

Tom chuckled. "We wonder about that from time to time."

"What are you guys talking about over dinner?"

"We're wondering, especially now since the FBI activity in Seattle, whether a plane would now be sent to Missoula from a different airstrip near Seattle. Also, we're wondering whether it would land at Missoula or at one of four minor airstrips in the area."

"It's an interesting thought. Thankfully, it's not a question I must address here in Camden."

"We're just talking here and eating dinner."

"Right. Stay out of trouble. Gotta go."

Erica disconnected.

Rick looked at Tom. "I guess she didn't want to talk about that, huh?"

"She doesn't want to involve herself in Missoula PD business."

"Yeah, that makes sense."

"You know, whatever we think or do or not do, the drug business in this area will continue as the demand and profits are a sure thing for the sellers."

"If these guys intend to use one of the minor airstrips near Missoula, they may want to employ a local Montana pilot to bring a plane in from Seattle."

"You're right," said Tom. "We have a lot of crappy weather and poor visibility when the clouds move in."

"With so much money at stake, these drug gangs will do whatever it takes to move their product. We get in their way; they'll take us out."

Tom nodded slowly. "I don't understand why Missoula, the FBI…why they aren't going after this gang."

"Maybe they are. It's just we don't know about it."

Chapter Twenty Seven

Becky is Afraid

The next day Tom stopped at the Fast Outfitter to buy feed and hardware. He waited until the customer at Becky's register had completed his purchase before he approached. He liked her and wanted to know her better. He was concerned that the smile she always gave him was missing.

"What's wrong, Becky? Are you okay?"

She tried a weak smile. "It's a family thing."

"None of my business, but can I help?"

She shrugged and then looked at him. "Well maybe. I was at a family get-together at my Uncle Antonio's place this past Sunday."

Tom nodded and she continued. "There was a guy there I didn't really know. He works at G&E. I remember someone a while back describing him as a gangster from Chicago. Anyway, later in the day, he and my uncle got into a serious argument. They went outside so not to upset the guests, but I could hear them from inside the French doors."

"Who is this guy?"

"His name is Tony Capone and he runs the business at G&E as the General Manager."

"What happened?"

"The argument seemed to center on my uncle's fear of what Tony was doing in promoting drug distribution from the G&E building; saying it would surely bring the Feds into their lives. Besides that, my uncle never liked the drug business and said he didn't want G&E involved in it. The argument got hot when my uncle brought up the subject of a dead DEA agent."

Tom frowned and shook his head. "Why are you telling me this? Aren't they like family secrets?"

"Yes, normally, but I'm frightened that something could happen to my uncle. I'm afraid this Tony guy might have my uncle killed so he can keep his drug racket going. I heard them argue about the dead DEA agent and the downed plane. My uncle was fiercely against whatever had happened. He demanded that Tony end the drug business at G&E immediately or he would close the plant. Tony was enraged and stomped off and left my uncle's home."

"Wow. That sounds like something serious."

"I don't know what I should do. I can't bear to think of my uncle murdered. I'm afraid to approach the police. Would they believe me? Would I be murdered for going against Tony? What do you think I should do?"

Tom saw the pain in her face and wanted to help her but was unsure how to proceed. "Stay calm, and don't do anything yet. Let me have a day or two to think about this. I'll get back to you."

"You promise?"

"A couple of days"

Becky smiled. "Thanks."

Startled by an alarm, Tom turned and watched a car drive up to his cabin. He leaned the spade against the corral fence and went to meet Rick as he got out of his car and waved.

"Hey, did you get some new wheels?"

"It's another rental. I hope I don't get firebombed again."

"I bet they weren't too happy with what was left of the last car."

Rick shook his head. "All kinds of paperwork. Then he grinned, "You said you had cold beers, right?"

"Sure, come inside."

Tom turned off the alarm that Rick had set off. They sat at the kitchen table, where Tom passed out cold cans of beer and set out a bowl of pretzels.

Rick took a long pull on his beer. He put the can down and grinned. "Okay. What's been happening?"

"I was talking with Becky yesterday at the Outfitter store. She told me this story about what she overheard when she was at her uncle's house. In case you've forgotten, her uncle is Antonio Giordano."

Rick shook his head. "You sure know how to pick 'em."

"Just listen and then tell me what you think."

Rick grabbed a handful of pretzels and leaned back in his chair. "Alright. Go."

Tom relayed what he had heard from Becky without comment and then turned to Rick. "Okay. You now know what I know. What do you think?"

"Holy cow. I leave you alone for a couple days and you go get yourself in trouble."

Tom scowled. "Yeah, I have a way of doing that. So, what do you think?"

"I wonder how real it is about her uncle possibly being whacked. He is the main man in that outfit, all be it he's way old. Do you think Tony has the stones for it?"

"It's beginning to look like Tony has quite an empire built up. He runs the drug business out of G&E but the profits are his. He's got a nice place with horses and real estate. I imagine any threat to his lifestyle would bring a quick and severe reaction. Becky thinks a lot of the old man and doesn't know what to do to keep him safe."

Rick grabbed another handful of pretzels. "What do you want to do?"

"I don't want harm to come to the old man. He's not running drugs. He has the old G&E packaging business that I think he bought for his nephews when they get out of college. Somehow, when he started the company, he had to take in some mobsters from Chicago; not sure why. Anyway, he's stuck with this dangerous Tony dude. The old guy may not be able to get rid of Tony. I think Tony is the one that runs the place. The old man threatened to close the place down rather than get in trouble with the Feds. Tony flipped out when he was told that, according to Becky."

"So, the old man might be at risk, I understand that. However, we do not have any levers we can pull at this time to help the old guy. Ironically, we have a pretty good idea who whacked the DEA agent, but here again we have no levers we can pull to have the Tony dude arrested."

Tom scowled and shook his head. "I don't like this impasse, it's not right."

Rick finished his beer and went to the refrigerator for another. He sat down and popped the tab open. "What do you propose we do? I know you've been thinking about this."

"I'd like to see Tony arrested for the two murders at the motel."

"Yeah, that would solve a few problems. But we first need proof positive of Tony's culpability before we make any move. We can't just hotdog it."

Tom nodded. "Yeah, you're right…or it will be us in prison."

"Okay, so what are you thinking?"

"I want to go up to the motel and to the truck stop next to it and look carefully for any video cameras that haven't been discovered by the cops, or maybe they just ignored. I recall there are a set of shops across the street as well. I want to map all the locations of cameras that might have captured Tony during this hit," said Tom.

"Even if there are cameras, you have to realize they have all been recorded over at least once by now, maybe several times."

"I know. I couldn't be that lucky. But if I can show where the cameras are that would have captured images of Tony doing the hit, then it might be enough for Tony to make a mistake if he thinks there are indeed images out there that could incriminate him."

"So, you're counting on the dude to make a mistake? That's your plan?"

"Well…won't he want to shift the blame…make it look like it was someone else did the hit?"

Rick shook his head. "If there are indeed other viable cameras and the dude can be convinced that his image was captured; well then, he might be worried. It's a tall order since there aren't likely anymore images. It's been too long."

"I'll have to check out these cameras and see if any still have the old images."

"Good luck with that."

"Let's get practical," insisted Rick. "What're you going to do if there aren't any more images? We have to get positive proof of Tony's culpability before making any kind of move."

"Is there a way to make him expose his own guilt?"

Rick sat back in the chair and drained the can of beer. "Could we dovetail into his e-mail accounts?"

"I know it's been done by some of the characters we were associated with in the past. That might be a question we can ask Larry."

"Okay," said Rick "Jump in my car and we can take a run down to Elk Creek."

"Let's do it."

It was well past the lunch hour when Rick and Tom arrived at Larry's Bar and Grill. There were still several patrons at the tables and several at the bar. Tom smiled at Diane behind the bar. "Is Larry available?"

She held up a finger and went to the office door, knocked, and cracked it open. A few words and Diane turned to Tom and waved him to the door. "He'll see you guys now." She smiled and went back to the bar.

Tom pushed open the door and Larry came from around his desk. He shook hands with both. "Hey, nice to see you guys. I was wondering what kind of trouble you've been into."

"You have a few minutes so we can run something by you?" asked Tom.

"Sure. Of course. Have a seat."

There was a knock at the door and Diane looked in. "Need anything?"

Larry looked at his two guests and raised three fingers. The door closed. "Okay. Let's hear about it."

Tom told Larry the same story he had told Rick.

Larry shook his head. He looked at Tom. "Sounds to me that you're getting yourself involved in another no-win situation."

There was a knock and the door opened. Diane brought in three frosty mugs of beer and then departed.

Rick spoke up. "We think it's a definite possibility that the old man will be hit as it doesn't sound like this Tony guy has any intention of shutting down his drug distribution. If the old man closes the plant, it will seriously impact Tony's operation. He'd have to set up a new place to handle the drugs."

"I'd like to keep the old man alive and tell Becky that no harm would come to him," said Tom.

Rick spoke again. "In order for that to happen we must find a way to neutralize Tony. Also, it really irks us that he will likely skate on the hit of the DEA agent. At least, we haven't heard anything about it from the FBI or anyone else."

"So, what is it you need me for?" asked Larry.

"Is there some way we can get Tony to expose his own guilt?" suggested Rick.

Larry smirked. "You mean because you don't have any real evidence?"

"We only have the very weak images of him at the hotel and at the truck stop. It's not much since we can't see his face well enough to make an I.D."

"So, you don't have squat."

Rick nodded. "Nothing we can use."

Tom added, "Okay. I agree. But if we get Tony arrested for the murders, he will no longer pose a threat to the old man…and I would feel a lot better having a murderer in prison."

Larry sipped from his mug and turned to Tom. "This may be obvious to you, but have you searched for any other possible cameras that might have caught Tony?"

"Rick and I were talking about it earlier. It seems since the event took place almost two weeks ago any recording would have been written over maybe several times by now."

Larry scowled and shook his head. "So, what you're saying is that you guys didn't actually check any other cameras; that any evidence is long gone. I have that right?"

Tom and Rick nodded. "We screwed up," said Tom.

"Dick Tracy you guys ain't."

"I'll go back to the hotel, see if there are other cameras," said Tom.

"Yes, do that and look at the truck stop as well. Meantime, I need to get busy and have Tony's e-mail cracked open. The whole operation might well be detailed out…might get lucky."

Rick pushed back from the table. "We appreciate your time, Larry."

"I'll check out any other cameras," said Tom. "Should we call you in a couple days?"

"Yes. In the meantime, you super sleuths need to get busy and not get in anymore trouble."

Tom and Rick thanked Larry and left the lounge.

In the car Tom looked at Rick. "I think we just got a spanking."

Chapter Twenty Eight
Video and Email

Tom stopped at a variety store and purchased several USB thumbs drives, then headed for the truck stop and hotel complex. He saw two cameras at the hotel, near where the dumpsters were located. Cameras were seen on both sides of the office entry. He did not see cameras in the lobby area. He inquired at the registration desk about access to the images from the various cameras.

The young attendant looked at Tom in an irritated manner and shook his head. "I can't let anyone back there. Besides, you're not a cop so forget it."

Tom pulled a roll of bills from his pocket and peeled off a ten-dollar bill. He pushed it across the counter toward the clerk.

The name tag on the clerk's chest read Roland Barrows. He glanced at the money and scowled. "Really?"

Tom pushed another ten across the counter towards the clerk who glanced quickly around the lobby and then indicated with a nod of his head for Tom to follow him. Roland led Tom to a narrow room behind the registration area. A large monitor screen displayed all the hotel cameras in an array. Roland pointed to a setup card pasted to the wall and then left the room and closed the door.

Tom fumbled with the computer to select the correct server and fidgeted with the controls until he figured out how to set the day and time parameters. He was surprised and happy that the server had an enormous memory. But rather than spend much time there; he copied the pertinent images onto a USB thumb drive. Twenty minutes later he laid another ten-dollar bill on the counter and left the hotel lobby.

He left his pickup parked at the hotel and walked to the truck stop and to the automobile fueling islands covered with metal roofing. He walked the length of the fueling facility and back to locate the various cameras mounted on the overhead shelter. There were cameras at the corner of the shelter at the gas pumps that covered the exit and entrance traffic. Tom thought it looked promising if only he could get access to the servers inside the office.

The manager of the facility was hesitant to allow Tom access to the camera servers. He wanted to get clearance from his boss who was not on the premises at that time. It took two twenty-dollar bills for Tom to get access to the room with the servers. Tom was awed at the sight of the many servers and recording equipment.

A six-foot cabinet with a glass door enclosed the equipment and Tom saw dozens of blinking lights on the servers. The manager showed Tom how to access each server from the computer at a desk with a large monitor. It turned out the recording equipment served cameras around the car fueling area, the truck service area, and many cameras inside the retail store. It took a few minutes for Tom to get the instructions to address the cameras he wanted to look at. As it turned out, the servers had huge recording capacity and held over 30 days of images. The manager was still very nervous and asked Tom to hurry. Tom copied the relevant images to the USB thumb drive and put a ten-dollar bill on the table as he left.

Back in his pickup he turned on his laptop computer and plugged it in to the power supply and connected it to the power outlet on his dashboard. The computer came alive. Tom looked through all the thumb drive images he had acquired from the hotel as well as those at the fuel pumps for the night of the murder. He was pleased to have snapshots of all vehicles leaving by the west driveway, the exit closest to the hotel. He found images of the parked gray Nissan on the night of the murder of the DEA agent. The images of the hit man were good, but not clear enough for identification. A partial plate number was visible.

Tom called Erica and asked her to get the name of the owner of the near new Nissan with the partial plate number. It only took a few minutes to get the name … It was Tony Capone.

Tom and Rick visited Larry in hopes that he had done some investigation on e-mail trails for Tony Capone. They weren't disappointed. Larry showed them a list of ill-gotten e-mail activity for Tony.

"Listen guys, this is confusing and hard to decipher. I'll continue to work on it. I'm sure I can get more useful information from this."

Tom shook his head. "I sure hope so. I can't make any sense of all this gibberish."

"I must caution you both. The information thus acquired is illegal and I will have to destroy it. So go ahead and look at it but leave it here."

"So, you have been studying this e-mail stuff," said Rick. "What have you made out from all this?"

Larry cleared his throat. "It seems to me that a guy named Ed Smiley is the guy to kidnap Antonio and make him disappear permanently. I haven't found where but there is a definite time-line of how it's supposed to happen."

"What else have you learned?" asked Tom anxiously.

"I found some personal information on this Smiley guy on the Internet, but I couldn't figure out his relationship to G&E or to Tony Capone."

"That's all you have so far?" said Tom.

Larry shrugged. "Very recent e-mail activity by Smiley suggested he would be going to a meeting at the ranch, and he requested this guy Burt meet him there; saying they both had things to do. Smiley sent instructions to Burt on how to get to this so-called ranch. Here, I wrote it down for you."

He handed Tom a folded note with the location of this ranch. As Tom looked at the information, he noted the ranch was located about 40 miles north of Missoula and 20 miles south of Camden, but within Camden County.

"Okay. I know what I must do."

Chapter Twenty Nine
Antonio Missing

Tom was brushing his horse when his cell phone buzzed. He set the brush aside and reached for his phone. The data window announced "Becky."

"Hi Becky, what's up?"

"I'm scared. I just received a call from the family in Missoula. It seems that my uncle has disappeared."

A chill went up his back. "Has someone called the police?"

"Yes. Yes. No one has seen him in a couple of days. He's not been well. I don't know what could have happened."

"Is his car still at his home?"

"No. It's at the G&E plant. I guess he was working at the office. But no one there remembers seeing him."

"Was anything unusual happening at the plant?"

"No. Don't think so. Just a regular day."

"Don't panic Becky. I'll call around and see what I can come up with."

Her voice broke. "I love that old man."

"I know you do. I'll see what I can find out."

Tom disconnected and placed a call to Rick at the newspaper. "Hey Rick, you have a minute?"

"Not really. I have a busted machine. Can you make it quick?"

"Yeah. I just got a call from Becky. She said her uncle is missing. Family called the cops down in Missoula. I told her I would see what I could come up with."

"What the hell can you do?"

"I'm going to explore the so-called old ranch down south of here that Larry discovered in his e-mail sleuthing. What Larry said leads me to believe that Tony may have grabbed the old man just to shut him up and take him off the board so the bastard can keep doing his drug business at G&E."

"Oh shit, you going to get yourself involved with those gangsters again?"

"You know how I feel about that creep, but I can't let the old man get whacked."

"Hell, he might already be dead. You're dealing with mobsters."

"Don't worry. I just wanted you to know what I was up to. I'll keep in touch."

"I can't leave here right now. You're on your own."

"No problem. I'll be in touch."

Tom called Erica to bring her up to date.

"Becky? Becky? This is about Becky...whoever the hell she is?"

"Yes. I told you…her uncle is Antonio Giordano. He's an old man, CEO of G&E."

"Am I supposed to be impressed?"

"That family is connected through Chicago. Those people assigned this Tony Capone to be the foreman at G&E. I suspect this Tony dude is the head of a narcotics operation in Missoula and connected to people in Seattle."

"How the heck do you get yourself involved in this bad stuff? Criminals? You have a death wish?"

"Erica, I talked to Rick this morning. He's tied up with some work problem. I told him Larry had discovered a place mentioned in some e-mail by Tony and his associates as a so-called 'old ranch' down towards Missoula but inside Camden County. Larry located the place on Google Maps and gave it to me."

"And how was Larry able to legally acquire the information from someone's e-mail?"

"I didn't ask, but he has all sorts of tools in his kit."

"Yeah, I bet he does."

"I just wanted you to know I'm heading out that way, to that old ranch, to see if indeed the old man is being held as a captive or worse. I'm going to leave my vehicle along the state road and approach the deserted old ranch through the forest on horseback. Getting close, I'll hide my horse and approach on foot. I'll call you after I've checked the place out and have an idea what to do."

"And what, you're doing all this for Becky?"

"I don't want the old man to be murdered...I don't want it to be on me. And yes, I'm also trying to help Becky."

"Tom, you're a fool. You should let my deputies investigate this. The Sheriff's Department and DCI should handle this. You shouldn't put yourself in a potentially dangerous or violent situation."

"Thanks, I understand. But I'm on my way and hope I can keep the old man from being killed."

"This isn't your fight." Her voice had calmed.

"The only problem I see would be if Tony Capone showed up. I'll call and advise you of the situation."

"Just to remind you, you have no legal protection and should avoid any confrontation. Instead, call here immediately. In the meantime, I will send two deputies to the location."

Tom gave her directions to the old ranch. He then called Rick and advised him of his plan and that he had talked to Erica. Rick said he couldn't leave work yet as they had a critical publishing issue to fix. Tom said he'd call him and keep him advised. He mentioned that Erica was sending two deputies to the location.

Tom took a pistol, carbine, and cell phone as well as a heavy tactical flashlight, first-aid kit, food, water, and a small sack of grain. Just before he left the house, he grabbed a group of cable Zip ties from the barn and stuffed them into his jacket pocket. Tom loaded his horse into the trailer and drove the highway to Missoula to stop at an obscure turn-off at the site of a gravel and stone business. Based on GPS data the old ranch was approximately four miles inland from the highway. He unloaded the horse from the trailer, saddled him and started down the narrow two-track.

Forty minutes later he came up to the old ranch. The place looked dilapidated, like it had been abandoned for a very long time. He called Rick and advised him of the location and told him the old place seemed abandoned with no one in sight. Rick said he was still at work as there was an issue getting the week's printing done. He said he would head toward Tom possibly in an hour. Then Tom turned his phone to silent ringing.

Tom hobbled the horse in the woods out of sight from the old building. It was after two in the afternoon and Tom made himself comfortable in clumps of spring grass in a stand of saplings. He watched the old building for any sign of a person and watched for the expected Ed Smiley and his cohort Burt to show up. It was after three when a car drove up to the cabin. One man got out and went around to the passenger side. He pulled open the door and pulled an old man out of the car. Tom could see the man's hands were tied in front of him and to his belt. They went into the building and the driver came back out to lean on his car and use his phone. Tom wondered if this was Smiley or the Burt fellow. He was sure the prisoner was Antonio. On further thought, he concluded that the driver was Ed Smiley.

Chapter Thirty

The Old Ranch

Thirty minutes later a pickup truck appeared on the narrow road with what Tom presumed was the Burt fellow.

A heated discussion ensued outside the cabin. Tom could not hear what was spoken. The two men then held a conference call on Smiley's phone with an unknown party. Finally, it seemed to Tom that Burt had given in to Smiley on the point of the discussion. Both Smiley and Burt examined their guns and put them under their belts at their backs.

Tom crept close to the back of the cabin and strained to hear what was happening inside. Then he crept away to hide himself in dense brush to the side of the cabin that would allow him to see anyone that drove up the road. He looked at his watch and wondered if Rick would be able to come and help him.

He knew he would have to restrain one of the two men quietly if he expected to get control of the situation before harm came to their prisoner. He was convinced they intended to kill Antonio. He seized on the idea of going to the pickup truck and turning on the headlights, waiting for Burt to come out, and then assault him there. But he knew he had to be ready to stop Smiley or the advantage would go to the two goons.

Tom back-tracked into the forest, moved quietly through the trees, then circled around the cabin to approach the pickup from the rear. He turned on the truck head lights and withdrew to the back of the truck as that offered a blind spot from the cabin. In his hand he had the heavy tactical flashlight. It was several minutes before Tom saw Burt leave the cabin, his gun visible in his hand as he slowly approached the pickup. He stood in front of the truck looking around into the nearby brush and trees. He stepped slowly to the driver's door and pulled it open, then stepped back.

Tom was coiled and ready to spring but caught himself in time. He watched as Burt looked toward the brush on his side, but then shook his head and turned back to investigate the truck cab. As he leaned on the seat to fumble with the dashboard switches, Tom pressed his gun against Burt's head. "Don't move."

"What the hell…?"

"Shut up. Don't move."

"Who the hell are you?"

Tom slapped his gun against Burt's head. "I said to shut up." He took a hold of Burt's belt and started to pull him face down out of the truck cab. "Slide out and shut up."

When Burt was face down on the ground Tom tied his wrists together at his back. He pulled the cable Zip ties snug. "It fuckin' hurts, man. What the hell you want with me?"

Tom slapped Burt in the head again with his pistol. "Shut up or I'll really hurt you." Taking his kerchief from his pocket he stuffed it in the man's mouth. "You're going to stay quiet." Burt nodded and grunted.

Tom left the truck door ajar and pushed Burt to the back of the truck and then onto his knees. He carefully looked around the truck bed to observe the cabin. He saw Smiley standing in the doorway looking around and focusing on the truck.

"Hey Burt. Where the hell are you? Hurry up."

When Smiley went back inside, Tom grabbed Burt by the collar and dragged him into the forest just past the truck. He hoped the dense foliage and saplings would offer concealment.

"Sorry buddy gotta do this." Tom wrestled Burt to the ground and tied his ankles together. Then he looped a tie through his wrists and his ankles to render the man unable to move. He repositioned the kerchief in his mouth and looped two ties around his head to keep the gag in place. Burt was writhing and moaning.

"Hey. Save your energy. I'll be back in a while."

Tom remembered his horse was waiting for him in the woods behind the cabin. Stepping quietly and quickly Tom crossed the road behind the truck and disappeared into the woods. A few minutes later he was by his horse. Tom unfolded a canvas cup from the saddlebag and emptied half of the water from his canteen into it. The horse drank it all in a matter of seconds. Tom quenched his own thirst and pulled the carbine from the scabbard. Thus ready, he quietly approached the side of the cabin and shielded himself in a thicket of saplings and watched.

He didn't have long to wait. Although he couldn't see Smiley at the front of the cabin, he heard him bellow.

"Hey Burt. What the hell you doin'?" After a few seconds Smiley yelled again. "Goddamn it. I'm coming out there…the old guy's not going anywhere. Hey! You hear me? I'm comin' out there!"

Tom kept looking at the corner of the cabin, waiting for Smiley to appear. When he did, Smiley acted confused. He kept looking at the truck and then into the forest.

"Burt, goddamn it! Where the hell did you go? What's wrong with you?"

Smiley took small steps toward the truck and then stopped and looked around.

Tom was ready to spring to the cabin door, but he would wait until he was sure to make it before Smiley could spot him. He was sure Smiley was armed and didn't want to offer him a target. It was almost a full minute before Smiley reached the driver's side of the truck and yelled. At that instant Tom made a fast dash to the cabin door and entered.

He couldn't believe his luck. Smiley was engrossed at the far side of the truck and continued to yell for Burt. Tom saw an old man huddled in a corner with hands and feet tied with rope. This had to be Antonio he surmised. He didn't look well. Tom didn't spend but a few seconds thinking about it. Instead, he readied his carbine and pushed the door closed but not latched. Still there hadn't been any challenge from Smiley. At the broken window Tom saw Smiley walking back and forth on the far side of the truck and calling for Burt.

Tom glanced at the door and knew what he had to do. When Smiley, still cursing a blue streak, turned toward the truck, Tom went to the door and flattened himself against the wall. He propped his carbine against the door jam and held his pistol at the ready. Just as the door burst open with a volley of cursing, Tom stepped out from behind the door and put his pistol against Smiley's head. "Hold it there. Don't move."

"What the hell…?"

"Get your hands up…way up."

Tom frisked Smiley and removed the gun tucked under his belt. He pushed the man farther into the room before kicking the door closed.

"Goddamn it. Who the hell are you, you crazy bastard?"

"Put your hands behind you." Tom jammed the gun against Smiley's neck. "Do it or I'm going to really hurt you."

He did as he was told. "What the hell you want with me? What've you done with Burt? Hey! You're fuckin' hurting me. It's too tight!"

"Tough shit. That guy you've got tied up in the corner probably doesn't like it either."

Tom shoved Smiley to sit him against the wall near Antonio who seemed to be only partially aware of what was happening.

"Tom was glad he had several zip ties left and he used one to tie Smiley's ankles together.

"What the hell you want with me? Who the hell are you anyway?"

"Tony tells you to off this guy or was Burt supposed to do it?"

Smiley stared at Tom in apparent confusion. "Who the hell are you? What're you talking about?"

Tom kicked hard at Smiley's foot. "You listening to me? If you expect to still be alive tomorrow, then you better start talking to me. Now, did Tony tell you to whack this guy or was that for Burt to do?"

"Goddamn it, where the hell is Burt?"

Tom reached over and slapped him hard across the face. "Talk to me, asshole."

Smiley licked his swollen and now bleeding lip. "I…I was supposed to bring him here. Where…where's Burt?"

"Tony tells you to off this old guy or was that for Burt to do?" Tom followed up with a brutal kick to the man's leg. "Speak up! Can't hear ya!"

"Goddamn you! Just supposed to bring him here. That's what he said."

"Who said? Tony?"

"Yeah, Tony. Who the hell else?"

"And then what? He's coming here?"

"Guess so. Don't know."

Tom slapped him across the face.

"You going to off this guy?"

"Stop…stop it. Maybe when he gets here."

"When? When's he coming here?"

"Before dark. He said before dark. Where's Burt? You kill Burt, you bastard?"

Chapter Thirty One
Tony's Goons

With the two gangsters now immobilized, Tom went to look at the old man. He found Antonio to have a weak heartbeat and shallow breathing. The man's pale face was covered in beard stubble. Tom noticed several needle marks on the right side of his neck and surmised one or more injections had knocked the old man out. He saw that the poor guy had relieved himself while unconscious. He stifled his rising anger toward the two men and went outside to check on his horse. He knew he'd have to hurry as Tony, or some other goon could show up anytime. The horse nickered, seemingly happy to see him. Tom brought the horse within sight of the cabin and hobbled it in a grassy area.

Tom brought Burt, while he muttered curses, into the cabin and secured his ankles again. Tom removed the gags from all the men but made sure they were securely tied. One hollered out, "Who the hell are you?" Tom didn't answer.

The phones of Burt and Smiley started ringing and went unanswered. Tom wondered if Tony had just then been alerted to trouble at the old ranch.

Tom checked again on the old man. "You beat up the old guy, didn't you?" He stared at Smiley. "Why did you have to do that?" Smiley shrugged and averted his glance.

It was almost 3pm when Tom called Erica and asked for assistance.

"What the hell is going on out there?" she asked.

Tom didn't answer but instead said that Antonio was not in good shape. "I think he's been drugged and beaten by one of these goons. He needs to go to a hospital."

"I can have an EMT sent down there."

"I have the kidnappers Smiley and Burt tied up. By the way, where are the guys you were sending down here?"

Erica said, "You are not deputized and could be accused of assault on those guys."

Tom lost patience with Erica. "I'm going to call DCI if you don't send someone to help with Antonio. Also, how about sending someone to arrest these goons?" Then he disconnected the call.

It was after four in the afternoon when Tom caught sight of a car creeping towards the cabin. It stopped a hundred yards away and was still partially shielded by trees. With this cautious approach, Tom was sure it was Tony or one of his men.

Meanwhile, the phone belonging to Smiley rang several times. After several minutes the car crept slowly toward the cabin. Tom could see only a driver and wondered if there were others hidden inside. The car was an older Toyota.

The car stopped near the old cabin at 4:30pm. The driver blew the horn many times and not getting a response left the vehicle and started yelling for his men. The phones of Burt and Smiley start ringing again.

Tom saw rope among the junk piled in the back of the cabin and knew it would come in handy. He hid behind the door as he had previously but now gripped an old whisky bottle. After ten minutes the driver walked cautiously to the cabin. He seemed wary of an ambush.

The man shoved the door open with the full force of his body against it. The force of the door incapacitated Tom momentarily. Tom dropped the bottle as he forced the door away from himself and back toward the intruder.

The man turned toward Tom with his pistol and fired once but missed. Tom grabbed the man's arm and viscously twisted the gun away from him as a shot went into the ceiling. Tom kicked forcefully to the back of the man's left leg and grabbed the gun as the man lost his footing.

Tom smashed the gun hard on the man's head. Now dazed and in apparent pain, the man was quickly tied with rope and gagged. Tom staggered from the exertion. His phone buzzed in his pocket, but he didn't answer it. He leaned against the wall gasping for breath and then went outside to recover from the exertion.

He realized the driver was not Tony and wondered who it was. Maybe Tony suspected a trap and had sent one of his goons.

Chapter Thirty Two
Sheriff Arrives

The sun was low on the horizon and shadows growing longer. Tom saw blue flashing lights coming down the narrow road through the trees. Two sheriff patrol cars pulled up in front of the old cabin. The car doors flew open, and four patrol officers jumped out and drew their guns and stood by their cars.

Their incoherent yelling of commands wasn't what Tom wanted to hear. He raised his hands and backed toward them. He bristled when cuffs were clamped on his wrists. The cacophony of commands was annoying, and Tom stood mute until the noise died down.

At that time Erica stepped out of a patrol car and walked up to Tom. She signaled the officers to release Tom and he stood there rubbing his wrists.

"You just can't help yourself, can you?"

Tom shrugged. "I wasn't going to let the old guy get killed."

"Because Becky asked you?"

"She knew I was interested in what was happening at G&E."

"At G&E, of course." She shook her head. "So, what the heck happened here? I saw your trailer out by the road."

"I rode my horse through the woods to approach the cabin from the rear. I hobbled my horse and watched the place for a while. It was after three when a car drove up and this guy Smiley got out and pulled Antonio out of the passenger side. The old man was tied up and could barely walk. The goon took him inside."

The patrol officers looked at each other and shuffled their feet. The guns were back in their holsters. Erica asked, "Is there more to this story? Who's in the cabin?"

"I was giving you the whole story. But the short version is that there are three bad guys tied up inside and the old man is still alive but not looking good."

"Oh jeez," she pointed to her sergeant. "Clear the cabin."

The four officers hurried to the cabin with guns drawn. Tom watched them as they entered. Soon an officer came to the doorway with four fingers raised. Erica's radio came alive as someone advised her of the situation inside.

"I think Antonio, the old man, needs a doctor," said Tom. "I'm sure he's been injected with something. There are needle marks on his neck."

She pulled a phone from her hip. "Is that what they told you, that he needs a doctor?"

Tom scowled. "I had trouble getting those guys to talk."

"Yeah, I bet you did." She started talking to someone at her headquarters and requested an ambulance.

Two officers marched the three goons out of the cabin. This time they were free of the Zip cords but were handcuffed. They were securely placed in the two patrol cars. One of the officers went back to the cabin with a bottle of water. Erica said the old man was to stay in the cabin until an ambulance arrived.

Erica turned to face Tom while writing in her small tablet. "I'm not going to ask you now how you managed to capture those three, but I will expect you in my office at nine tomorrow morning to give a full accounting."

Tom nodded. "The three goons report to Tony Capone. They expected him to come here to deal with the old man, but I think he knew there was trouble when he couldn't get anyone to answer his phone calls."

Erica shook her head. "Fascinating. Nine tomorrow morning."

"Got it."

She walked off toward the cabin.

The phone started buzzing in Tom's pocket.

"Hey, Tom, it's Rick. What's been happening?"

"Well, I'm all set to leave here and go home. Erica and her officers showed up."

"I've been working all afternoon getting the equipment running here. I haven't heard anything. What happened down there?"

"The short version is Antonio was a prisoner in this old cabin. There were two goons guarding him and a third arrived later. I managed to get one at a time tied up and called Erica to come deal with it. She resisted but I threatened to call DCI and she relented."

"So, she's there now?"

"Yeah, her and three officers. Ambulance coming for the old man."

"Hey, I have to get the whole story. I'll catch up with you tomorrow."

"Okay. I have a meeting scheduled with Erica at nine in the morning. I'll call you after."

"Yes, I want to hear all about it. Maybe something for the paper?"

"Sure. I'll call you."

Tom asked the officer guarding two of the thugs for a bottle of water. The officer reached into the car and handed him one and went to the other car to check on the third prisoner. Tom walked back toward the cabin and retrieved his hobbled horse. He offered the horse water by pouring it into a cupped palm. He saved the last for his own parched throat. Then he climbed on and trotted back up the narrow road toward his truck. He didn't look back.

At nine the next morning, Tom was seated in Erica's office. She turned on a recorder as her conversation with Tom began.

"Okay Tom. I've spoken with Missoula PD this morning and gave them an update to what happened at the old ranch."

Tom coughed. "All of this happened in Camden County…"

"Of course, but since it involves people from Missoula and Tony Capone, it is important to keep the Missoula people informed. Now, I want to record your official statement as to what happened at the old ranch. Please start at the beginning and don't leave anything out."

Tom spoke slowly making sure he included all details of the events at the old ranch. Afterward, Erica went over some items to extract more details that Tom had glossed over. It was a half hour later when she turned off the recorder and sat back in her chair.

Erica shook her head. "This one-man crusade of yours could result in a lawsuit by the three suspects. You were not deputized after all."

Tom shrugged. "I'd do it again in similar circumstances."

"Yeah, that's who you are." She moved some papers around on her desk and then looked at Tom. "Missoula PD hasn't been able to find Tony for an interview, not at home or at G&E. An arrest warrant has been issued for him for conspiracy to kidnap and assault. By the way, the three goons are here in our facility; however, the ADA in Missoula is preparing indictments against the three for kidnap and assault. Meanwhile, they remain in jail here without bail."

"What's the story on the old man?"

"Antonio Giordano was in Camden Hospital but has been transferred to a rehab hospital in Missoula by the family."

"Well, I guess we're done here. I'm going to meet up with Rick and get some lunch."

"Erica looked at Tom and then smiled. "Take care of yourself."

Tom nodded. "Thanks."

Chapter Thirty Three
A Cold Shower

As noon approached, Tom and Rick met at Joey's Diner.

"So, it went okay with Erica?" asked Rick.

Tom nodded. "We went over all that happened at the old ranch. She wanted to get all the details on a recorder."

"Really? Is she afraid higher-ups will be asking questions?"

"That's what I think. I didn't question it though, just went along with it."

The waitress appeared with their cheeseburger platters and coffee. They both started in on their generous pile of French-fried potatoes.

"She said there was an arrest warrant issued by the ADA for kidnap and assault for dear old Tony," said Tom. "I hope they catch him soon. I don't want to be looking over my shoulder all the time."

"I wonder what's happening at G&E with the old man not there and Tony hiding somewhere. Somebody has to be running the regular business…and what about the drug business at G&E? That was Tony's thing."

Tom shook his head. "I've no idea if the FBI or DEA have any interest in the drug business at G&E. I would have thought those guys would have been all over it by now."

"It sure is strange. What could they be waiting for?" said Rick.

"I still expect Tony to be arrested soon for the probable hit on the DEA agent and his lady friend at the hotel. There's got to be many FBI agents looking into it even if we're not hearing about it."

"I have permission from the paper to come up with a follow-on story covering the events at the old ranch," said Rick.

"You're going to be stirring up a hornet's nest. You want to do that?"

"It's a real story. It's what I do."

"Okay. You need to make sure you don't leave yourself open for an ambush."

"I'm doing that. Well, good to talk to you," said Rick. "I better get back to the office."

"Yeah, I still have work to do to get the corral water system finished. Stay safe."

"You too."

Tom pulled up in front of Fast Outfitter. He needed hardware to complete the watering system in his corral. He hesitated a moment before getting out of the truck and wondered what kind of mood Becky would be in. He hadn't called her since their date, so he was expecting a cool reception. He liked Becky, but there hadn't been enough sparks to set off a romance. Well, he'd be cordial and maybe it would go well, he thought as he got out of the truck

After a minute he found what he was looking for, solid brass fountains that a horse could activate while pushing with its nose. He then picked up other hardware to make draining fixtures in preparation for winter. As he approached the rear counter, Becky looked up and gave him a brief nod and grin. She had rung up Tom's purchases before either spoke.

"Haven't heard much from you," she said. "Everything okay?"

"Sure. What do you hear from your uncle, Antonio?"

Becky placed Tom's purchases in a sturdy bag. "He's now at home with daycare and guard service. The family is worried about his safety. He is feeling well, though."

Tom handed Becky his charge card and then signed the receipt.

"I appreciate all you did to help my uncle."

"How are things at G&E now since Tony is on the run?"

Becky shrugged. "I don't know anything about it." She quickly turned to serve another customer.

It was obvious to Tom that he had been dismissed. As he left the store, he realized he should have called her at the very least. He would have to make it up to her in some way.

When Tom stopped his truck in front of his cabin, he saw a note stuck in the door jam and wondered who had left it there. When he opened the folded note, he was surprised to see it was from Lisa. She and her mother had stopped by, and she was very sorry to have missed him. Nervous emotions stirred in him as he realized how much he missed her company. The previous year had been tumultuous and had brought them in danger from criminals, mine collapse and their own fragile emotions. They both had come to realize they cared for each other dearly, but he hadn't allowed their feelings to overwhelm them. After all, he was so much older than she, who was then still a teenager. But now, over a year later, he was having second thoughts. Maybe a cold shower would help.

Chapter Thirty Four

Rick in Danger

The next morning, as he prepared his breakfast, the intruder alarm sounded. Looking out the window, he saw a SUV drive into the yard and stop in front of the cabin. As the passengers got out of the vehicle, he spotted the FBI patches on their jackets. He turned off the alarm and opened the door to strong knocking. These were agents he had not seen before. They introduced themselves and claimed to be following up on what they had read in the local paper and wanted to hear what Tom knew about the involvement of Tony in the kidnapping of Antonio, and whether Tom could provide additional information on the involvement of Tony with the murder of the DEA agent. The three men had a long conversation about Tom's experience and speculation regarding what Tony was involved with. The FBI agents expressed serious interest but then only shook their heads in disappointment with the lack of proof positive to Tom's allegations.

That evening Tom stopped in front of the newspaper building to pick up Rick as they had planned to have supper at the diner. As he watched Rick leave the building several shots rang out from well behind where Tom was parked. Rick fell to the ground. Tom leapt out of his truck with his pistol in hand. Not seeing anyone and not hearing any more shots, he pocketed the gun, pulled out his phone, and called 911. At Rick's side he tried to stop the bleeding with his kerchief and steady pressure. The shot had gone into his left abdomen.

"Rick! Rick! Talk to me…Ohh shit. Rick, help is coming, Talk to me."

Tom couldn't get a response from Rick. Fear permeated through him as he thought Rick was in a dire condition. Just then a deputy sheriff arrived and a minute later an EMT ambulance arrived. There was a frantic effort to stabilize Rick and then take him to St. Patrick's Hospital. The deputy asked questions of Tom as he tried to jot details in his notebook.

"I gotta go to the hospital…I gotta go."

The officer nodded and put his notebook back in his pocket. "Yeah, go ahead. I'll catch up to you."

As he rushed to the hospital, he received a phone call from Erica who wanted to hear what had happened. Tom gave her a quick update and said he'd call her later as he was almost at the hospital.

It was a long night of waiting at the hospital before Tom was allowed to see Rick. Apparently, the bullet had done serious damage. The doctor seemed hopeful that Rick would recover with a minimum of lasting issues. When they took Rick to ICU, Tom was allowed to sit with him for a short time. Rick was barely conscious but acknowledged Tom with a tortured smile. Tom said he would return the next morning.

As he was leaving the hospital, Erica arrived. They sat in the lobby while they had a short conversation about Rick's condition and the circumstance of his shooting. Rick had been shot with a pistol. There had been no witness to the shooting, and she was not hopeful for a quick resolution. As he got up to leave, Erica cautioned him about doing something irrational and advised him to work with the sheriff's department. He nodded and waved as he left.

Trying to get some sleep, Tom struggled with what had happened. He assumed the attempt on Rick's life was a response to the article he had published in that morning's paper. Rick had not heeded earlier warnings about his bombed-out car from a yet unidentified caller. Tom knew Rick had a stubborn streak and wouldn't let it go when he recovered. Tom assumed the efforts to quiet Rick had come directly or indirectly from Tony Capone. Rick's articles had laid out with some probable certainty the events starting with the murder of the DEA agent and his date. Then, there was the involvement of G&E in the disbursement of the recovered drug cargo from the crashed plane, and the impact of the information that he and Rick had discovered about the G&E facility. Now, the exposure of Tony in the assault and kidnapping of Antonio in the probable attempt to force G&E to be a drug conduit against the wishes of the old man, Antonio, had been detailed in the last editorial article. Tony had to realize this sort of exposure could ruin him and his business, thought Tom, and surely the gangster would do whatever he had to to prevent it. Tom realized he too was a target for Tony. The event at the old ranch would have removed any doubt about it.

He realized the alarm system and video cameras surrounding his cabin area, although helpful, were not a guarantee that a determined assault could be prevented. The only solution now would be to take Tony off the board. How to do that, he pondered?

The next morning Tom entered St. Patrick's Hospital at ten and asked for Rick's room number. The room light was dimmed, and Tom walked quietly to Rick's bedside and stood looking down at his friend. An array of dials and displays were evidently monitoring Rick's condition. He looked to be sleeping and Tom sat on a chair waiting for him to awaken.

Rick awakened an hour later and grinned at Tom.

"How're you feeling, or shouldn't I ask?"

"I'm still in a lot of pain but all my functions are working…I think they are." He grinned at Tom who shook his head.

"I guess neither one of us saw the shooter, huh?"

"Sure didn't."

They both agreed the attacker had most likely been one of Tony's henchmen.

"I guess poking a stick in Tony's eye wasn't a good thing to do. We're both guilty of it."

Rick nodded. "We have to come up with a new tactic to get that bastard to trip up and give the law something to hang around his neck."

"I don't think the violence will stop until Tony is taken off the board."

Rick shook his head. "Careful what you're thinking."

"Antonio is being cared for at home with a guard," said Tom. "Also, Erica mentioned there was an arrest warrant out for Tony by the Missoula PD."

"Really? That's good news."

"Yep, for kidnap and assault. Tony hasn't been seen since the day of the kidnapping."

"I gotta ask you Tom, not to get involved with this incident. I'll be up and at 'em soon. Just lay low and let things calm."

"I'll be careful…for now."

Chapter Thirty Five
Bomb Roust

Tom received a call from Becky Durance at Fast Outfitter. She had heard part of a discussion at her uncle's house that had alarmed her and wanted to give Tom an update. Antonio was in guarded seclusion at a nursing home, his health still not well. Everyone at her uncle's house was aware of the arrest warrant for Tony. However, no one was sympathizing with Tony, and all agreed not to be involved with him. They all agreed with Antonio not to sanction Tony's involvement with the Seattle drug gang and that running drugs was not something the family wanted to be involved with. The friends agreed the Feds would find and arrest Tony soon. All agreed bringing FBI attention to them was bad for the family.

Tom called Erica and repeated what Becky had told him.

"Becky again?" said Erica chagrined.

Erica assured Tom the FBI would pursue Tony for assault and kidnapping of Antonio and the Missoula PD would look at G&E management for possible drug trafficking. She also assured him the FBI was pursuing the DEA murder case, but new information was not presently available.

Tom, however, wasn't convinced FBI or anyone else would pursue Tony for the murder of the DEA agent and the hooker. He visited Rick at the hospital and saw a guard present in the hallway. Rick was still in pain but looked better. Tom told Rick of his conversation with Erica.

Rick said he understood Tom's angst with the murder of the DEA agent but cautioned to let the Feds deal with it. He cautioned Tom that he is likely a target for Tony and his gangsters due to his involvement with the Antonio rescue as well as his interest in the drug transport into the area.

A nurse came into the room and advised Tom that she will be giving Rick another sedative and Tom should leave.

Tom went home and started working again on the automated watering setup in the corral for his horse. He made sure the system could be turned off and drained for the winter season, as a freeze-up would cause serious damage.

As Tom stood up to stretch from his cramped work position, he saw a figure standing where his narrow driveway came out of the trees. He squinted, clearing his eyes to be sure of what he saw. He had disabled the alarm system when he left the cabin to avoid tripping it and having to run inside to disable the loud horn.

He could see it clearly now, a stout man with baseball type hat and tan field clothes scanning the area with binoculars. Suddenly the man disappeared.

Tom moved quickly into the barn where he picked up his pistol and shoved it under his belt. He walked through the barn and out the main door, but he no longer saw anyone where a minute ago a man stood with binoculars. He stood quietly and listened but there was no sound of a car engine, only the rustle of aspen leaves in the breeze. He questioned whether to chase after the man but was almost certain he would be chasing a ghost long gone into the forest. He swore with several angry utterances and recalled the caution Rick had suggested earlier.

Back in his cabin, he put a pot of beef stew on the gas range and reheated the coffee. He reset the alarm system and looked at several monitors from cameras he had attached to tree limbs. He was sure the intruder was long gone, but wondered what devilment awaited him now.

During dinner and afterward, he watched TV with an eye to the alarm panel. He knew a determined and experienced intruder could defeat the alarm sensors and this worried him now more than usual.

Sometime after 9pm he went to the barn to check on his horse and give him some human company. He brushed him thoroughly which the horse seemed to appreciate. Later he went to bed with his pistol under his pillow.

He awoke several times during the night. Finally, he arose at 6:30am and made coffee. Mug in hand, he went out to feed and check on his horse. Then while he leaned on the barn door and sipped his coffee, he let his eyes scan the area at the tree line. His attention went to his pickup parked by the small corral north of the cabin. The driver's door was just slightly ajar. Had he left it that way he wondered? No. He would *never* leave the door ajar.

Had someone installed a bomb in the cab? He was frightened. He didn't dare touch the door. He called Erica who put him in touch with a bomb expert at DCI.

It was almost an hour later when officers from State Police and DCI arrived. The State Police bomb removal expert had brought a bomb-sniffing dog that immediately sat down at the driver's side door. The bomb expert lay under the driver's side of the vehicle for what seemed like an eternity. Meanwhile, everyone was made to move far from the vehicle and the bomb technician donned his protective gear. Then he went first to the passenger door and spent a few minutes partway in the cab. He then went to the driver's door and slowly opened it. There was no explosion. The technician removed items from inside the cab and placed them on the ground. He then removed his protective suit.

Tom saw Erica as she drove up the hill and into his field as the State Police and DCI people were cleaning up from the bomb removal. Officers were in conversation with Tom as they took information for their reports. Tom saw Erica in conversation with the officers before she approached him. She was shaking her head as she came up to him.

"Life is sure exciting with you around. Someone was serious about getting rid of you."

Tom smiled and nodded. "It was close. I noticed the driver's door on the truck was not closed tight. I *always* close it tight. Always. That scared me and I called you."

"And who do you finger as the culprit?"

"I have good reason to suspect one of Tony Capone's goons. As you know, there is an arrest warrant out for Tony regarding kidnapping the old man."

"Plus, all the other stuff you have accused him of," said Erica.

Tom nodded, "That too."

"No one's seen Tony since that kidnap event. Missoula PD is very interested in arresting him for the kidnapping and associated assaults."

Tom scowled. "Too bad we can't add attempted murder with this bomb attempt."

The radio on Erica's shoulder came alive and she turned to Tom. "I have to get going. I sure hope you can manage to stay alive, you and Rick."

"Thanks for your help."

She waved and walked to her vehicle.

A few minutes later the State Police and DCI officers also departed.

The next morning Rick called Tom and asked him to come by in the afternoon as he would be dismissed then to home. He had argued to go home as opposed to a rehab hospital. Finally, a doctor had reluctantly agreed.

Tom entered Rick's room just after 3pm. An orderly was helping him get ready to leave. When the orderly left, Rick turned to Tom and exclaimed, "How the hell come you didn't call me and tell me about the bomb? For crisakes, you should have called me."

Tom shrugged. "I was going to call you last night but then I fell asleep. This morning I got your phone message, but I decided to tell you now. Didn't want to distress you."

"You're not telling me *distressed* me. I had to hear it from Erica. So, what the hell happened?"

"After I saw you yesterday, I was doing some work on the watering system at the corral. When I stood up, I saw a guy with binoculars over in the trees where my driveway enters the yard. I didn't chase him, just figured he'd be long gone by the time I got to where he was. I set my alarms and went to sleep late with my gun under my pillow."

Rick grumbled and shook his head.

"The next morning, I was sipping my coffee outside when I noticed the driver's side door of my pickup was not closed all the way. I always, always, close the door solidly. It's a thing with me. Anyway, it scared me. I called Erica and she got hold of the State bomb guys and DCI and they came over. Their dog sniffed out a bomb and they worked a while to find it and remove it. I'm sure glad they got it out of there."

"For crisakes! And you didn't call me? I had to hear it from Erica?"

"Yeah, sorry. I didn't want to distress you."

"That pisses me off…had to hear it from Erica."

Tom picked up Rick's bag of hospital items and turned to the door. "Come on. Wheel your ass out of this room."

In the hallway Tom gave the bag to Rick and started pushing his wheelchair toward the entrance.

"Rick, are you allowed to stay home by yourself? Maybe stay at my place for a few days?"

"I told them I'd be home. I'll be fine. There's a follow-up nurse that will come by every day for a week. I should be okay by then. I want to work on my computer; there's lots of stuff for me to do for my job."

"Well, you know you can stay with me."

"Appreciate it. Thanks. I'll be fine." Rick chuckled, "Besides, it's too dangerous at your place."

"You have a point there."

Chapter Thirty Six
Becky is Missing

Erica called Tom the next morning just after 10am. "Hi Tom, you awake?"

"Sure, I'm awake. Second pot of coffee."

"I received a call from the manager at Fast Outfitter to report that Becky did not report to work. He said calls to her phone went unanswered, went to voice mail."

"Damn, what else?"

"I sent two deputies to her apartment and was told her car was still there. Based on the seriousness of the situation I authorized the deputies to force an entry. However, the door had not been locked."

"Strange."

"The deputies reported that Becky was not in her apartment. Her purse was on the floor near the door. Her keys and phone were in her purse. Some furniture and accessories in the living room were disheveled seemingly of a physical encounter. There were no traces of blood found."

"Oh Jesus, someone's grabbed her."

"Looks that way. I had my two detectives examine the scene. They haven't reported back to me yet. I'm about ready to call DCI."

"You might talk to Becky's relatives in Missoula and see if they might know where she is."

"It's on my list. I'll call them now."

"Do you know if Tony Capone has been arrested yet?"

"No one has seen him according to my last call with the Missoula PD."

"Has anyone interviewed Becky's friends at the Fast Outfitter?"

"Like I said, I have my two detectives working it. I'm sure they won't miss it."

"Do you know whether Antonio Giordano is safe?"

"I've been told by the deputy on duty that no visitors have been by."

There was a pause and then Tom said, "I'm beginning to wonder if maybe Becky was kidnapped as a ruse to get me in a vulnerable position so Tony's thugs can take me out. I'm certain Tony and his thugs want me and Rick dead. I'll give Rick a call."

"Be careful. Don't go off the handle on me."

"I'll be in touch. Thanks."

Two hours later, Tom received a call on his cell phone from a muffled male voice. The data display indicated "Unknown Caller."

"Hello."

"Is this Tom?"

"Yeah. Who's this?"

"I've been told that we should meet so nothing bad happens to your friend."

"We should meet and do what?"

"I'm told you and the boss have to come to some understanding about current events in order to keep everyone in good health."

"And just who the hell are you and who is this boss you speak of?"

"I don't want to say anymore on the phone, but I'm told you are well aware of whom we're talking about."

"Okay. We can meet at the Sheriff's Office," said Tom.

"Don't be ridiculous. We can meet in the parking lot of the library."

Tom knew the parking area and the library itself well. Two sides of the parking lot abutted a forested area, one side bordered the street and the other side edged against an office building parking area. Tom recalled seeing cameras located at the corners of the building at the eves and guessed it might provide coverage across half of the parking lot.

"Alright. I'll be in the center of the parking lot within an hour. You or whomever will have to show me proof that Becky is unharmed."

After a few seconds the man agreed and disconnected. Tom assumed the phone was a non-traceable 'burner' and decided against asking for a trace. Instead, he drove immediately to the library in Camden. There were cars in the parking lot, and he chose a parking spot that he hoped would be inside the security camera's range. He checked his gun and put it in his jacket pocket. He got out of his truck and leaned against the fender. He had no idea how long he would have to wait and decided he would leave after twenty minutes.

It was almost fifteen minutes when he saw a maroon Buick enter the parking lot. The car had dark tinted side windows. The car stopped some distance away facing him. After nearly a minute, the car drove slowly to where Tom was parked and stopped two parking spots away. No one got out of the Buick for over a minute and then a man left from the back passenger door and walked slowly to where Tom stood. He carried a phone in his hand.

"Who the hell are you?" said Tom. He had a hand in his jacket pocket.

"I'm your friend on the phone. Name is Gary. You must be Tom, right?"

"So, prove to me Becky is okay. Is she in the car?"

"Relax, all in good time."

"So, who's in the car? Let's get this over with."

"We have to get something straightened out first."

"Yeah? Like that?"

"Boss says you and your buddy have been harassing him and sticking your nose where it doesn't belong. Now I'm just the messenger, so listen up. Boss says you and your buddy stop all harassment in person and in newspaper and forget he even exists, and all will be forgotten."

"Really? Where is Becky?"

"Have you been hearing me or what?"

"Anything happens to Becky – anything – and you won't believe the shit that will rain down on your boss. Are *you* hearing me?"

"Boss, he doesn't want to hear this."

"Where's Becky?

"She's fine for now."

Tom looked at his cell phone display. This number where I can reach you?"

"Yeah. What you want I tell the boss?"

"I suggest you listen carefully. I don't give a crap what you tell your boss. He will soon have to pay for the murder of the DEA agent and his friend and the kidnap and assault of the old man. And add to that the kidnap of Becky. Also, there'll be a big federal rap for the transport and distribution of narcotics. The only way you can possibly save *your* ass from what's going to happen to your boss is to come clean to the sheriff or DCI. Otherwise, you and your buddies that work for this boss will go down with him."

"Wow. No kidding?"

Tom pulled his phone from his pocket. "Should I call the sheriff for you now?"

The thug quickly got back in the car, and it sped away. Tom memorized the plate number.

He pressed the button on his phone to call Erica at the Sheriff's Office.

"Hello. Tom?"

"Hi. Yes. I was just approached by some goon named Gary in a maroon Buick." Tom told her the plate number. "He apparently was speaking for his boss, which would be Tony, I'm sure."

What did he want from you?"

"Basically, he said for me and Rick to stop the harassment and he would leave us alone. I couldn't get him to say where Becky was."

"I just checked on the plate number. It's a stolen plate."

"Of course, it is. You haven't heard anything about Becky?"

"Not yet. I alerted the Missoula PD. No response yet."

"I don't know what to think about all this," said Tom. "Is she still alive?"

"How did you leave it with this Garry guy?"

"Well, I was losing my temper. Told him anything happens to Becky all hell would come down on him."

"Oh boy, that will surely get his cooperation."

"Yeah, well, that's what happened."

"And what is it you want me to do?"

"I just want to go on record, I guess."

"Okay. Done."

"Thank you."

Erica had hung up. Tom swore. Things weren't going well. What had happened to Becky? She was Antonio's niece; could they have hurt her? Did they dare? Did the Missoula cops have the situation in hand? Not likely. No one's heard from her. What could he do? He had to do something. She was in serious danger from that Tony bastard. There was no doubt the Chicago thug would remove any obstacle to his criminal operations at the G&E plant.

Tom picked up the phone and called Rick. "Hey Rick. I gotta call from this Gary guy, part of the Tony gang. He's holding Becky somewhere and wants you and me to promise to stop harassing Tony. The alternative unspoken was he'd kill us; maybe Becky too."

"Who is this Gary asshole? What's he done with Becky?"

"He's holding it over me; wants a promise to leave Tony alone, not cause any legal trouble."

"I hate to say it, but Becky could already be dead."

"Damn it, don't say that."

"Just saying. Tony is a nasty bastard from all I know of him."

"Yeah, the cops here and Missoula are looking for him for a whole host of charges."

"The guys in Chicago, who put him in charge down here, I'm sure, wanted a low profile so they could count on profits from the drug operation and not a lot of problems with the law."

"What are you thinking should be my next move?" said Tom.

"Well, if we were back in the day, I'd say to take him off the board before he does us."

"My sentiment exactly. Meanwhile, the law is already looking for him. Maybe I can help them out."

"You mean, *we*," said Rick.

"Probably couldn't do it without you."

"First thing we need to do is find the bastard and maybe keep him on ice for a while."

"Where would he have Becky? She's his leverage with the old man," said Tom. "I hope we can get her out of harm's way."

"Have you checked out Tony's place recently?"

"Just that one time," said Tom. "Would he keep her so close to home?"

"Otherwise, he would have to rely on his goons to hold her somewhere while he continued to evade the cops. If I was him, I'd keep her close."

"Yeah, his crew is more testosterone than brains."

Chapter Thirty Seven
Finding Becky

Rick hadn't recovered completely and complained frequently of pain. But he had insisted on being Tom's driver. Their plan was for Tom to approach on foot to reconnoiter the grounds and buildings in Tony Capone's estate. When they arrived in Missoula, Tom directed Rick to a secluded grove of trees west of the estate where they parked. They didn't see anyone in the immediate area. Several horses grazed in the field.

"How're we doing this?" asked Rick. "What's the plan?"

"I want to sneak into both barns and see if Becky is there and whatever else I can discover."

"Aren't they pretty close to the house?"

"Yes, we have to be careful…don't want anyone to see us and call the cops."

"Yeah or fill our ass with buck shot."

"Uh-huh. That too." Tom pointed to the heavy horse fence they were approaching. "Let's climb over here and walk up the barn. If we stay in the heavy brush along here, we should be okay."

There wasn't anyone out and about. The horses looked curiously at them, but otherwise were not alarmed. The brush along the fence had not been cut in a long time and offered good cover to allow them safe passage to the barn farthest from the house. It was a sunny warm day and they heard no one and no machinery. The barn was fitted with two hinged and heavy doors. When Tom unlatched the doors, he slipped into the barn without incident. Rick followed immediately and they closed the doors quietly.

Their nerves took a jolt as a cat went scurrying away. They noticed that there was a separate room at the far end of the barn, and they headed there. The barn was empty except for a small tractor and a large amount of garden tools. They walked quietly to a door to the separate room. Tom pushed the door open slightly and then hesitated.

"Holy cow!"

Rick tried to see past him. "Is this what I think it is?"

"Sure, as hell isn't horse feed," said Tom.

They were looking at what they were sure were stacks of packaged drugs.

Rick swore. "It looks like maybe cocaine and fentanyl. I can't be sure."

Tom shook his head. "I wouldn't want to be the one to handle that fentanyl stuff."

"Me either. Let's get the hell out of here."

"Yeah, no sign of Becky in here. I want to look in the other barn."

"I hope we don't run into a dog," said Rick. "I'd have to dispatch it really quick."

"Yeah. Let's take a quick peak in the other barn and then get away from here."

Not finding any sign that Becky was around the Capone property, Rick started the drive back north to Camden with Tom.

"Well, we didn't find any trace of Becky," said Tom, "but on the other hand that's good news."

"Yeah, they've got her hidden somewhere, though. They want to use her for leverage."

Just then Tom's cell phone started buzzing. He pulled it out of his pocket and looked at the display. "It says 'Unknown Caller'."

"Must be your bookie," smiled Rick.

"Hello."

"This is Gary. Remember me?"

"Yeah. What the hell you want?"

"I thought maybe we could help each other."

"You did, huh?"

"Yeah, I got to thinking about what you said the other day."

"Really? What'd you have in mind?"

"I heard direct from the man, he wants you and your pal dead and soon."

"No shit, what else is new?"

"He said he was afraid if he was arrested you and your pal would make it go bad for him."

"He's right about that," said Tom. "By the way, where is Tony?"

"I don't know where he is now. He moves around a lot."

"You're just a font of information, aren't you?"

"I could cooperate if I got relief from the law."

Tom chuckled. "Why are you proposing this now?"

"I don't want to be arrested for murder and that's what's going to happen according to Tony, and kidnapping the old man was bad enough."

"The bastard is right about that. Why the hell haven't you gone to the law?"

"I just found this out last night. I'd go if you supported me as I doubt anyone would take me seriously. And, if the word got out down here, Tony would kill me for sure."

"Tell me where Becky is."

"He had her at the G&E facility for half a day but now both are gone. Missoula PD has been at G&E twice looking for her."

"I want to know where Becky is."

"I won't say where Tony might have gone with Becky. I don't want to be part of whatever is happening to her."

"And what, you expect me to help you?"

"All I'll say is he might be using a cabin in the woods. If you can get me some relief, I can help you more. Bye."

Tom looked at Rick. "What an asshole."

"It sounds like this guy is looking for a way out."

"Or it's some sort of trick," said Tom. "I don't know."

The next day Rick showed up at Tom's cabin with a hard-shell equipment case.

"Hey, check this out." Rick opened the case to display a drone and controller.

"Wow. That must have set you back some."

"Cost me a couple grand two years ago. It comes with a big battery so it should give us the range we need to check out the old ranch before we show up there to some hostile characters."

"Sure, the monitor will let us survey the whole area."

"You bet. We can zoom in close while still at altitude. Nice, huh?"

"This is freakin' awesome. Let's take a run down there. I have to know if Becky is a prisoner there."

"Okay. You drive."

"I'll park the truck off the road just before reaching the stone purveyor place."

"Okay," said Rick. "I'll launch this bird from there. It has plenty of range."

"Yep, if it looks like the place is vacant, we can drive in there and check if Becky is being held in that cabin. I'll go in to check the cabin while you stay with the drone."

"Yeah, I'm still in some pain."

Later that day, before reaching the stone purveyor place, they parked out of sight of the road. Rick launched the drone from the truck and controlled it with its computer and display unit. Rick worried that he had never flown the drone very far and wondered if the cabin might be farther than its range. But they found the cabin on the monitor and made several passes at low elevation. There was no vehicle observed in the area and the noise of the drone had not caused anyone to leave the cabin. At this point they retrieved the drone and Tom drove down the rutted two-track to the cabin.

They stopped about fifty feet in front of the old ranch and waited to see if anyone left the cabin to inquire of their presence. They sat there for five minutes without seeing anyone. While Rick stayed with the truck and kept the engine running, Tom put a gun under his belt and left the truck. He dashed to the corner of the cabin and waited a few seconds before going to the closed door with his gun now in hand. In one swift motion he unlatched the door and kicked it open. It took a few seconds to be able to see into the darkness. There was no one and nothing of consequence to be seen in the large room. But he had the one bedroom to check before leaving. He went slowly to the bedroom door, unlatched it, and pushed it open.

There on the bed lay Becky, tied and bound to the bed frame with a gag over her mouth.

"Becky! God, I'm so glad I found you."

She was conscious and uttered strange noises from under the gag. Her eyes were tearful but sparkled with obvious relief.

Tom quickly took out his Leatherman from his pocket.

"I'll have you lose in a minute. Lay still 'till I get these things off of you."

Working quickly, he cut through the tape and cord that was used to restrain her and removed her gag.

Becky hugged Tom and suddenly burst into tears. None of what she said made sense to him. He vigorously rubbed her ankles and wrists and then helped her to her feet. She quit her rambling talk and started to cry again. He helped her to the door and then out to the truck.

It occurred to him that time was not on their side as some of the gangsters could show up at any time. He picked her up and placed her in the front seat with Rick and then sat next to her. The three of them were talking at the same time but finally she was able to tell them what had happened as Rick drove slowly back toward the road. The tension was high as they feared encountering one of Tony's crew on the narrow track. But they reached the county road without incident and sped toward Camden as Tom called Erica.

Chapter Thirty Eight

Trouble Arrives

They drove rapidly toward Camden as Becky told her story. She had been kidnapped when she arrived at her apartment at the end of her workday by two goons that worked for Tony. She had been taken directly to the old-ranch cabin. Tony was there but had only a few derogatory words for Becky and then left.

Arriving in Camden their first stop was the Sheriff's Office where Becky told her story to Erica. Becky declined medical attention and asked only to go home. Erica said she would be the one to take her home, but first she had to be examined by a doctor. Becky insisted it wasn't necessary, but Erica said it was protocol and not up for discussion.

Before taking Becky to be examined, Erica called Detective Dave Pritchard of Missoula PD and repeated the story told her by Becky and Tom. They discussed preparing arrest warrants for Tony Capone for the kidnap, imprisonment, and assault of Becky. The warrants were to be issued immediately. When Erica drove Becky home, she assigned deputies to 24-hour guard duty until further notice.

Meanwhile, Tom and Rick went to Joey's Diner for dinner and to discuss what to do about Tony since he posed an imminent danger to both. They realized Tony, a Chicago mobster, would not let them survive to be able to testify in a court room, and certainly not willing to let two 'home boys' ruin his life. Since the Missoula PD and now the Camden County Sheriff had issued arrest warrants for him, Tony had been unable to conduct drug business or legitimate business at G&E. He had been in hiding to avoid being arrested. Tom and Rick feared that Tony would try to kill them as soon as possible and they needed to take immediate precautions.

Rick stayed that night with Tom at his cabin. They took turns on watch and at 2:45 in the morning the trespass alarm sounded, and the external lights turned on. Tom took a quick look at the alarm board and saw that the trespass alarm had been tripped just at the entry to the meadow. A look at his outdoor infrared camera images showed two figures standing still at the edge of the meadow maybe confused by the bright lights they had tripped.

Tom and Rick, now armed, left the cabin using the rear escape door. Both went into the woods and past the north corral to be even with the two trespassers. Tom couldn't locate the trespassers at first and had to move away from the blinding effect of the bright lights.

At that time, he realized there were three men lower down the driveway toward the road. That would be five men total he surmised.

Tom and Rick found hiding places in the woods where they would have clear views of the advancing trespassers as they topped the slope and entered the well-lit part of the meadow. It was ten minutes before the three intruders were seen at the north end of the meadow and the five now stood in a group.

Then, the first man advanced along the wooded east edge of the meadow parallel to the cabin. The second man moved quickly across the meadow to stand by the small corral north of the cabin. That left three men at the entrance to the meadow. Tom and Rick could see they were using handheld radios.

The second man quickly made a torch from something he carried and then moved past the north corral to the cabin. Tom was not going to let his cabin catch fire; he would shoot the man if he had to. The man prepared to throw the torch as Tom carefully aimed and pulled the trigger. The man yelled and fell to the ground and appeared to curl up in pain. Tom had aimed at his shoulder, hoping not to have to kill him. The torch burned out on the ground.

After the first shot, Tom called 911 and reported the situation. Two minutes later, Erica called back to assess conditions and said she was dispatching two deputies immediately and would also arrive with another. At the same time, shots rang out from the first man across the meadow, shooting in Tom's general direction, but Tom had rolled immediately after his shot. More shots ring out by a third man who was standing at the entrance to the meadow and now made a dash to where the man with the torch had fallen. He picked up the torch and tried to light it. Tom's next shot felled him also. The torch remained unlit.

At that time Tom and Rick saw the beams of headlights coming up the slope to the meadow. Rick moved to position himself more able to cut off anyone trying to go back down to the road. A Jeep appeared suddenly, now illuminated by the bright lights at the meadow. The Jeep had a blinding big light bar on the roof. Tom and Rick could not see who was inside until the light bar and headlights were turned off. The vehicle did not move for at least thirty seconds and then the passenger door opened. A man of average height got out and Tom immediately knew from his stature and dress that it was Tony Capone.

Tony started walking slowly but purposefully across the meadow toward Tom's cabin. The Jeep kept pace beside him. A hundred feet in front of the cabin it stopped. The driver left the vehicle and walked slowly with gun in hand toward where the two wounded men lay on the ground occasionally moaning in pain. Tony stayed by the Jeep as his companion reached the two wounded men and examined their injuries. He said something to Tony who barked an order.

The driver picked up the torch and started to light it. When it was burning well, Tom heard Tony yell the order to throw it. It was then that Tom pulled the trigger. The man crumpled to the ground and the torch flickered out. Tony uttered a yell of rage and got into the driver's seat of the Jeep. He turned the vehicle around and went rapidly back to the north end of the meadow. There he stopped and his two uninjured men came up to him and gathered at his window.

At that time sheriff's deputies roared up the slope to Tom's meadow with blue lights flashing. They stopped on entering the meadow, only fifty yards from the Jeep. Time seemed to stand still as Tom watched the event before him from the darkness of the trees. He could not see Rick hidden in the trees but knew he was close to them. Two deputies left their vehicle and with guns drawn approached Tony and the two other men. Tom saw the three raise their hands as one of the deputies approached them. He saw them drop their guns on the ground and step back as ordered.

While the deputies put handcuffs on two, the third suddenly and viciously smashed his fist into the nearest cop's face, stooped down, picked up a gun, and was quickly swallowed up in the darkness of the dense trees just outside the area lit up by the brilliant lights. The other cop was startled as he handcuffed the first of the group and had reacted slowly to the situation. Tom saw that Tony had escaped and could not believe how fast it all had happened. Tom called Rick on the two-way, but Rick did not respond. Tom could see now that the two men were cuffed and sitting on the ground near the Jeep. The cop that had let Tony get away stood there rubbing his injured face.

Chapter Thirty Nine
Tony Escaped

A Sheriff's SUV roared up the hill onto the meadow and into the glare of the bright lights. No one moved for a few seconds and then the doors of the vehicle opened. Two deputies climbed out and Erica stepped out of the driver's seat. The deputies immediately went to assist the officer attending to the two prisoners.

Erica called Tom on her cell phone. "We're here. Where the hell are you two?"

"We're in the shadows in the trees. Didn't want to interfere with what was happening."

"Oh yeah, I bet. How about you show yourselves and get over here?"

Tom and Rick left their hiding places and walked out of the dark forest into the floodlight lit area of the meadow. They joined up as they approached Erica standing by her SUV. They could see the look of exasperation as she shook her head at their unhurried approach.

"Well now, I'm sure you have an explanation for all this hell raising." She looked at Tom and nodded. "Suppose you start. I can't wait to hear this."

Tom turned to point down the meadow toward his cabin. "We've got some casualties."

She strained to investigate the near darkness toward the cabin. "You've got what?"

"I called 911 when the trouble started."

"Run through it again form me. I didn't get all of it. Casualties?"

Tom gave Erica a quick summary of the violent encounter with the arrival of some of Tony's goons, and the shooting of three of them in their attempt to burn his cabin. Then deputies had arrived. He described what happened when Tony himself showed up and that he had escaped capture and was on foot in the forest.

Erica called DCI for assistance as she walked toward the injured hoodlums. She asked DCI to expedite the arrest warrant for Tony Capone. She quickly ascertained that the three men shot by Tom were seriously injured and she called for EMT help. They arrived within eight minutes.

A few minutes later a SUV with two DCI officers came up the hill onto the pasture. Together with Erica they interviewed everyone but got nowhere talking with the thugs. The DCI officers placed them under arrest and took them away. Tom and Rick waited until the hoodlum's vehicles were towed away and the meadow turned quiet again before addressing Erica.

"You two realize there will be a real investigation here, don't you? You better get some legal advice while you still have time."

Tom shrugged. "Right now, I'm more concerned about what Tony is up to. He wants me and Rick dead, one of the goons said so. We need to find him."

"I will have my deputies scouring the woods this evening and into the morning. He'll turn up."

"I can't sleep with him running around trying to burn me out."

"Listen, both you guys come into the office in the morning. I need official statements from you for the record."

Tom and Rick nodded. "We'll be there," said Tom.

"Come in. Have a seat. I'm going to record your statements and I don't want you to leave anything out."

"We're ready," said Tom. "Let's do it."

Erica scurried around setting up the recorder and organizing her paperwork.

Rick asked, "So what happened last night. Did you find Tony?"

"Did you arrest him?" asked Tom.

She shook her head. "I had two deputies looking up and down all the back roads, but there was no sign of him."

"Damn it," said Tom. "Where the hell is that guy? I can't have him loose to burn me out of my cabin."

"I don't know if maybe he had some help getting out of here," said Erica. "He could be hiding out somewhere."

"Well hell, I can't go to sleep in my cabin with him on the loose."

"I understand," said Erica. "We'll keep looking for him. I'll ask DCI for some help."

Tom shook his head and turned to Rick. "Think you could spend some time at my place at night. I don't know what else to do at this point. That asshole is coming back for sure."

"Yeah, I'll come by every evening before dark…until he's caught."

"Alright guys, let's get this statement done."

Tom and Rick, no sooner were back at the cabin than the phone rang.

Tom grabbed the phone before checking who was calling. "Hello."

"Hi Tom."

"Lisa?" Tom saw Rick roll his eyes as he went to the refrigerator for a couple of beers.

"Nice to hear your voice. I'm off from school today."

"It's good to hear from you. What have you been up to?"

"I called mainly to tell you that I saw a guy as described on the TV loitering near where my parents live."

"When was this? Last night?"

"No. It was this morning early."

"What was he doing?"

"Nothing. Just hanging out, obviously waiting for someone."

"Just standing there?"

"He walked back and forth in and out of the trees and then a dark blue pickup came by around 7am and picked him up."

"What about the pickup?"

"Too far to read the license. It was a white guy driving. Sorry I can't tell you anymore."

"Thanks Lisa, I appreciate it. I'll talk to the sheriff."

"Okay. Nice hearing your voice."

"Me too." Tom hung up and turned toward Rick.

"She saw a dark blue pickup this morning around 7am pick up a stranger hanging out near her parents place."

"Sounds like our guy. Probably eluded the cops by staying off the roads all night."

"Damn. I wonder where he is now?" said Tom.

"He's probably still around here somewhere. He has to get rid of you and me…has to."

"I better call Erica. Let her know about the sighting."

Rick nodded.

Chapter Forty
Tony Loses

It was just past noon; Tom and Rick were at Joey's Diner.

"There's been no sign of Tony from what I've heard," said Rick.

Tom shook his head. "I'm afraid that he's thoroughly enraged, and he won't stop until he kills me or burns down my cabin. The asshole that works for him said as much."

"We've got to see that guy in prison or dead in order to get some peace."

"I think Tony is going to get some of his goons to make trouble for us and burn my place down. He can't afford to be seen out and about with an arrest warrant active."

"An attack by his goons will be impossible to foretell and for sure they'll target your cabin."

"I'm not leaving home without being armed," said Tom.

"Me neither. I've asked permission from the lawyers at the paper to write an article about the event at your place to include names. I expect to hear back by tomorrow."

"Tony will be coming after you too, for damn sure."

"I have the article ready to go. If I get a go-ahead, it'll be published in Camden and in the Missoula News that very day or the next."

"I expect that article will bring out Tony's goons in full force," said Tom. "They'll want revenge."

It was 8:30am when the phone rang the next morning. Tom picked it up as he was preparing breakfast. "Hello."

"It's me again, Lisa. I'm on my way back to campus and stopped at the Exxon station just west of town. I saw the same man fueling up an SUV… the same guy I saw by my parent's place a couple days ago."

"Is he still there? Can you call the sheriff?"

"No. He drove off after I pulled in. It was the same guy, I'm sure."

"Appreciate your calling."

"Thought you'd want to know. I gotta go. See ya."

Tom called Erica.

"Hey Tom. Kind of early, isn't it?"

"Maybe. Lisa was on her way back to campus just now when she spotted the guy, she saw by her parent's place yesterday. She swears it's the same guy."

"Where was this?"

"The Exxon station on the west side. But the guy drove off. He was in an SUV."

"So, you think this Tony guy is hanging around Camden? Why would he do that?"

"Looking for me, I expect."

"I've got two deputies in town now. I'll have them look for him, but I'll bet he's long gone."

"Okay. Thanks."

Depressed at Erica's lack of real interest, he hung up. He stared at his breakfast and then pushed it aside.

During the week Tom spent time repairing the barn and riding his horse in the pasture and the woods. He went outside armed. When he checked with Erica a couple days later, she said that she hadn't heard of any sighting of Tony. Tom was wondering when Tony would come for his revenge. He was living as a fugitive and Tom knew Tony blamed him for his situation. Something would happen, but when?

It was almost noon on Friday when Tom was awakened from a nap by the ringing of the phone in the kitchen.

"Hello."

"You sound sleepy. It's noon time."

"Erica? Yeah, taking a nap. What's up?"

"Hey, listen up. My deputy was called to a shooting at the Exxon station just a while ago. A man had been shot twice through the passenger window of his SUV. Both shots were into the side of the head. The shooter escaped on a motorcycle."

"Wow. Do you know who the victim is?"

"Deputy said the victim was identified as Tony Capone of Missoula."

Tom nearly dropped the phone. "No kidding? It was really him?"

"The victim was identified by picture ID he had on him. It's him, Tom. It's Tony."

Relief overwhelmed him. "This is great news! Who the hell shot him? Do you know?"

"We don't know. It sure looks like an assassination."

"Maybe his Chicago bosses got tired of his screw-ups that put them in a bad light, especially if he were to get arrested and then talked."

"Makes sense to me."

"Thank you for telling me. It is really good news."

"Should make sleeping a bit less stressful."

"Thanks again."

"See you."

When Erica hung up Tom felt an overwhelming relief. He picked up the phone again and called Rick at the newspaper.

"Hey Tom, what's up?

"Got a call just now from Erica. Our boy Tony is dead.

"No kidding? What the hell happened?"

"A shooter on a motorcycle put two bullets in his head while he was at the Exxon station."

"That's awesome news. His people had enough of him."

"You and I can relax a little now," said Tom.

Chapter Forty One

Lisa

It was the following Tuesday and Tom had just sat down for lunch when he heard his horse neigh in the corral. He put down his cup, grabbed his pistol, and bolted to the window. His heart jumped into his throat.

"Lisa," he gasped.

He turned off the intruder alarms and then watched her, in shorts and halter top, lithely slip off her unsaddled horse, allowing him a stirring view of thigh and buttocks. Her auburn hair streamed down her back and swirled about her in the breeze. He recalled the first time he had seen her, and now over nineteen she didn't fail to arouse. After a tumultuous year of gangsters and danger he had come to respect and adore her. She was not just beautiful and arousing but an intelligent, brave, and caring person that had won his heart.

When he opened the door, she was in his arms. "God, I missed you so much." Her kiss lingered uncomfortably to where Tom gently pushed her away.

"Mom drove me here a couple times, but you weren't home. I was so sad."

"I'm glad you're here. I think about you a lot…more than I probably should. Are you off for the summer?"

"Not really. I signed up for some summer classes. They start next week."

"So, when do you start at Missoula?"

"Hopefully in the fall."

"I'm sure glad you're doing so well and making progress. You'll have a business degree in no time."

"My parents and I are very grateful for the help you're giving me."

"It's you are doing all the work. Anyhow, I'm about to fix lunch. Do you want to join me?"

She wrapped her arms around his waist. "Thought you'd never ask."

As he closed the door and moved to the gas range, Lisa brushed him aside.

"Sit down. Let me do this. Okay?"

Tom grinned. "I was getting stuff ready."

"Please. Just sit down. I'll do this."

Tom sat at the table and took a sip from his coffee cup. "It's so good to see you again."

She didn't look at him, busying herself with sausage and eggs and preparing toast. "I think often of us…the other year…of how things were."

"We're both a little older now."

"Uh-huh. But the feelings are the same…for me."

"They are for me too. I often catch myself looking down the meadow… expecting you to appear out of the forest like a spirit."

"I wish things had been a little different for us."

"I know. I'm so much older…"

"That didn't matter to me. Still doesn't."

She ladled scrambled eggs and sausage onto their plates. She placed the pan back on the stove, ran her fingers through his hair, and sat down. "Are you going to eat or just stare at me and make me upset."

"Lisa, I…" There was a knock on the door. He realized he had turned off the intruder alarm. They looked at each other. He shrugged and went to the window.

"Damn."

"What? Who is it?"

He reached for the latch and pulled the door open.

"Erica…"

She stood at the open door looking past him to Lisa at the table.

"You have company…"

Lisa gave a half-hearted wave.

"We were just having lunch," said Tom.

Erica scowled. "Playing house, are we?"

Tom coughed nervously. "Would you'd like some coffee?"

She turned her back to Lisa. "I'll pass on the coffee. Just came by to tell you the AG out of Helena will be in my office tomorrow at nine. She's going to review all that's happened regarding the shootings and the demise of Tony Capone. I need you there to answer any specific questions she might have. Can I count on you?"

"Sure. I can be there."

"Appreciate it." Erica turned and left them, walking swiftly to her state SUV.

Tom stood at the doorway and watched her enter her vehicle.

Lisa approached Tom and wrapped an arm around his waist. "She could have called."

"Uh-huh."

Erica droves away, tires spurting gravel as she accelerated.

"She's always had a crush on you."

"I don't encourage it."

"I know."

"She's the sheriff now and I'd like to stay on her good side."

"I actually think she's a good person."

"You and she had some tough going in the mine collapse."

"Wasn't sure either one of us was coming out of there."

"You helped her stay alive."

"We all did our part." She moved to stand in front of him. "I don't want to, but I need to be going."

"It was a pleasant surprise to see you."

Lisa smiled. "I think of you often, maybe too often." She went to her horse and with a smooth motion she was on his back. With a subtle shift of her body the horse was carrying her down the meadow to disappear into the forest.